The Farm on
Nippersink Creek

The Farm on Nippersink Creek

JIM MAY

August House Publishers, Inc.
LITTLE ROCK

Published by August House, Inc.,
P.O. Box 3223, Little Rock, Arkansas, 72203,
501-372-5450.

Printed in the United States of America

LIBRARY OF CONGRESS CATALOGING-IN-PUBLICATION DATA
May, Jim, 1947–
The farm on Nippersink Creek : stories from a Midwestern childhood / Jim May.
p. cm.
ISBN 0-87483-339-6 : $18.95
1. Spring Grove Region (Ill.)—Social life and customs.
2. May, Jim, 1947– —Childhood and youth. 3. Country life—Illinois—Spring
Grove Region. 4. Spring Grove Region (Ill.)—Biography. I. Title.
F549.S696M38   1994
977.3'22—dc20   94-1930

First Edition, 1994

10 9 8 7 6 5 4 3 2 1

Executive editor: Liz Parkhurst
Project editor: Kathleen Harper
Assistant editor: Jan Diemer
Design director: Ted Parkhurst
Cover illustration: Nancy Seidler
Typography: Peerless Lettergraphics

This book is printed on archival-quality paper which meets the
guidelines for performance and durability of the Committee on
Production Guidelines for Book Longevity of the
Council on Library Resources.

AUGUST HOUSE, INC.   PUBLISHERS   LITTLE ROCK

To Shorty and Agnes

Acknowledgments

I'D LIKE TO THANK MANY PEOPLE, more really than I can in this space. Ruth Sawyer said it takes three elements for storytelling to exist: a story, a storyteller, and someone to listen. I make my living telling stories, face to face, and I am grateful for the audiences who have invited me into their imaginations and lives, who have, in fact, participated in the creation of many of these stories.

I was fortunate to grow up in a community where visiting, or "neighboring" as my mother called it, meant that anecdotes and stories were shared as a part of everyday life. I am indebted to many people of my parents' generation—wise elders who have shared their memories and told me stories. They include Jim Haldeman, John McDonald, Tommy and Lorette Madden, Clara Vogel, Franklin Stevens, my aunts Mayme Hoffman, Delores May, Margaret Weber, and Alice Weber, my Uncle Art Kattner, and Mel Seidler. Thank you all for your sense of history and your perspective.

Stories were common in my family. My brother Paul was renowned for his humor. On construction projects, he would park his road grader under a tree at lunchtime, and the men would come from all ends of the job to hear his jokes and stories. It always made me proud. My sister Georgia, the oldest, would go to town for the free movies that were projected on the side of the hardware store. At home her brother and sisters would sit on the roof of the chicken house while she "told" them the movie. My sisters Donna and Diane were my first storytelling audience. I was five years old and had the run of the farm all day. They'd come home from school and ask me, "So what did Sonny, Tony, and Harvey do today?" It was my duty then to create a story about my three imaginary friends—I still work best under pressure. My sisters listened, and my storytelling career was born.

I'd like to thank Jimmy Neil Smith and NAPPS (National Association for the Preservation and Perpetuation of Storytelling) for sharing the vision so freely. Thank you, Ray Hicks, for telling me about Jack. I am perhaps most grateful to a community of professional free-lance storytellers who have welcomed, inspired, and challenged me over the years: to Jackie Torrence and Doc McConnell for providing the spark; to Barbara Freeman for her kind and thoughtful critiques and support in those early days; to Ed Stivender because he was the NAPPS board member who stood at the edge of the front porch, late at night, listening to us, practicing his devotions, while most had gone to sleep; to Jay O'Callahan for never letting me forget the importance of what we do; to Donald Davis for showing that you can start at home; to Michael Parent and Beth Horner, who suggested that I make storytelling my life's work; and to Milbre Burch, Len Cabral, Michael Cotter, Elizabeth Ellis, Bill Harley, David Holt, Larry Johnson, Susan Klein, Dan Keding, Gwenda Ledbetter, Syd Lieberman, Andrew Leslie, Bobby Norfolk, Connie Regan-Blake, Gayle Ross, Jon Spelman, Joseph Sobol, the late great Gamble Rogers, and many others; it has been a joy to walk this way with you.

Special thanks to my editors at August House: to Kathleen Harper for her enthusiasm and for letting the stories into her heart, and to Liz Parkhurst for seeing this project through to completion with skill and insight and for understanding my sometimes odd creative rhythm. Thanks to Dr.

Joyce Hancock for her vision and for her comments and advice, and to Jennie Bartoline for her careful proofing and suggestions during the critical final stages of writing.

My love and fondest admiration to Nancy Seidler, who has always believed in this book, and whose own artistic vision graces its cover.

Contents

Introduction

I WAS BORN ON A SMALL ILLINOIS DAIRY FARM, population seven. When I turned eight, we moved into the village of Spring Grove, population two hundred. By my sixteenth year I was tired of farms and small towns. I longed for movie theaters and places where teenagers could dance, and I detested being called a "hick" by the more urbane and cosmopolitan kids from McHenry (population three thousand at the time). At eighteen years of age I escaped—entering the University of Illinois, population forty thousand, and majoring in Russian History and Urban Problems.

Now I live close to home, in a barn, alongside a small stream that forms the headwaters of Spring Grove's own Nippersink Creek. I make my living telling stories, and I am artistic director of the Illinois Storytelling Festival, which brings storytellers from all over the world to Spring Grove. Likewise, of course, it is that small community that provides the setting for this book. Storytelling has brought me home.

Mary Kurtzman, a teacher of mine, once speculated that if every person had a computerized diary into which they recorded the important life events of each day, and if through some miracle of technology and human consciousness, everyone could, on a daily basis, read the diary entries of every other person in the world—the joys, sorrows, triumphs, tragedies, and honest reflections—then war and hatred would end.

This seems too much to ask of the simple process of telling one another our life stories. But, to some extent, stories do define relationships. We tell a co-worker just a short bit of our story—perhaps what we said to the policeman who issued us a ticket on the way to work. With our friends and family, we tell of our struggles, hopes, and plans for the future, and with those best friends, close family, and life partners, we tell just about everything.

Jay O'Callahan says that we live in narrative. Ed Stivender prefers to think of the act of storytelling as a dance—and how that man can dance! I think of telling stories as an attempt to establish community, whether it be one person telling another something important or funny, or a performer telling a tale to a thousand people in a theater, the success of the interaction is always determined by the extent to which a community has been formed on the spot. You can feel it in your skin.

And so to you, dear reader, I present the community that raised me. It is a community that can never be again, and it is one that never quite existed the way that it is pictured here—owing mostly to the filter of memory, my desire to tell a good story, and perhaps my own fears and shortcomings. Nevertheless, I offer these narrations in the hope that you and I can meet somewhere in this book, that on one of these streets, or cow paths, or maybe along the creek bank, we can pause, see each other, and swap a story.

Spring Grove

Spring Grove's landscape is dominated by St. Peter's Catholic Church, a colonial red-brick building with wooden columns and a steeple of stark white. The steeple rises above the small village, with its many oaks and willows, like a white heron standing watch over the equally numerous ponds and creeks. The church was built in 1900 and in its simplicity and choice of materials would be a suitable Protestant house of worship on any street in America. But in fact, its construction was inspired and necessitated by German Catholics who grew up in Johnsburg, a small settlement along the Fox River to the south. Some of these first-generation Illinoisans moved three miles north to a basin formed by the Nippersink Creek, built a mill, and started farming. They wanted a church close to their farms, businesses, and taverns.

Spring Grove's founders did not build so grand a church as the one left behind. Johnsburg's was a Gothic edifice complete with an adjacent churchyard that contained the graves of parents and grandparents who had left their churches in Germany and come to till the black soil in the valley of the Fox.

The new church in Spring Grove had none of the European flair of its Johnsburg counterpart. Its neat austerity reflected, perhaps, the lighter purses of these younger, American-born families, if not the prairie farmer's preoccupation with survival and the necessities of life. Nevertheless, it was and still is Spring Grove's most splendid building.

To it the families came to mark the passing of the seasons and of their lives. They came to celebrate, to worship, and to mourn. Here a father would come on a winter's morning to grieve the death of his daughter the night before—prayerful but with a heart forever stabbed. Through the heavy fog in his soul he would pray, trying to understand the taking of so much, at such a young age. The church was the place to ask for comfort and for divine explanation.

Over the years, the people of the town came dutifully to the church to mark the great events of their lives. The bodies of men and women would lie in cool, gray slender caskets surrounded by six-foot candles in the same building where they had been baptized. Pallbearers would carry them down the same aisle that they had walked as brides and grooms, their legs strong and eager for the journey ahead. After the wedding mass, long tables were set up in the church basement for ham, roast beef, German potato salad, jello molds, homemade dinner rolls, and fresh pies. After most everyone was good and stuffed, the tables would be cleared and the celebration would become uproarious with polkas, fox trots, and too much beer. Sometimes during funerals, you thought you heard the music of the dance band coming up through the floor.

Meandering in front of the church in a slow, muddy, purposeful waltz was the Nippersink Creek—the ancient mother of the verdant glen and the pagan soul of the village. In its thick, amber waters swam alligator gar, whiskered catfish, bullheads, and water snakes. In the spring it was a roaring torrent of foaming water and driftwood, while in late summer it barely moved, its slow, shallow silence broken only by the deep, bovine echoing of bullfrogs. The creek's murky depths inspired generations of children with its mystery and forbidden possibilities.

My family has lived here since the 1840s. My father was born in 1896. He was once proclaimed the waltz king of McHenry County.

His friend Tommy Madden told me so. Tommy was eighty-six at the time, and we were sitting in the living room of his small home—a room that had once displayed hats in this turn-of-the-century storefront house. The late winter sun painted the brown hills and oak trees orange and yellow. But there was a cold edge to the February air. Winter dies slowly in the northern Midwest; it's hard on the old people, fixtures on the land who are unable or unwilling to go south. In Tommy's hoarse voice and cough there was a yearning for spring, when he and Lorette would go for car rides to see old friends and to seniors' luncheons. In the summer he'd leave the door open to the fresh afternoon air and watch the Cubs on TV.

"Your dad loved to dance!" Tommy explained. His eyes brightened, and a wry smile started on his stubbled ruddy face. And so began the story.

Dad and his friend Ford Hanford had been to a dance in Twin Lakes, just across the Wisconsin state line. They were returning home to my grandparents' farm in the early morning. There were no dance halls nearby to speak of, and it was a long way by horse and carriage. Sometimes it was a matter of driving the buggy all night, arriving home just in time to put the horse away and to milk the cows. Spring Grove was a long ways from everywhere and still is. But in those days, when my father was a young man, the loneliness had to be eased by horse and buggy.

That night, my father was driving Grandpa's black pacer. My father was proud of that pacer horse. Indeed, pacers were well thought of because of their speed and the smoothness of their gait, the way they could move down the road. They were considered the best buggy horses of their day.

Now my father loved horses and had a horse-trader's sense of mischief. Next to driving an easy-moving carriage horse, there was nothing that he liked better than to play a trick on a neighbor. As the tired dancers bounced along Wilmot Road nearing home, they noticed that Jack Warner had his black trotting horse let out to pasture. Jack had recently moved into the tenant house on the Carey place and had a a trotting horse identical in size and color to Grandpa's pacer. Naturally, Dad thought it might be a good idea to swap horses on old Jack there in the moonlight.

He pulled Grandpa's horse to a stop, took its harness off, and tied it to a nearby tree. Then he and Ford caught Jack's trotter. They harnessed it and hitched it to their buggy. They turned the pacer loose in Jack's pasture and headed home—a fine ending to a night of dancing to fiddle tunes, laughing with the farm girls, and sipping hard cider.

As the story is still told in Spring Grove today, Jack Warner got up before sunrise like any good farmer. In the dim light, he hitched his farm wagon to what he thought was his black trotter and drove into Spring Grove. He stopped at my grandfather's general store and, with a considerable amount of controlled excitement, told everyone, "By God, my horse has learned to pace overnight."

When the light spread from the eastern horizon across the prairie, each of the small farmsteads came to life with the sounds of roosters crowing, cattle and horses stamping their feet on the ground, and back doors slamming as the farmers made their way to the barns. In the morning light, Jack Warner recognized that the horse he had tied to the hitching post there at Nick Weber's general store was not his own.

It was reported that Jack was mad, but not for long. Chances are his angry words became chuckles soon enough with the help and encouragement of amused friends at the store. For these moments of laughter were welcome ones that helped pass the time and broke the spell of the hard, tedious work.

And being tricked meant that Jack was recognized as a member of the community. It meant that his neighbors would milk his cows if he got sick, and that friends would turn out to rebuild his barn if it burned down. And of course, being tricked meant that he'd become part of a story that in turn would become a small piece of the fabric of the town, told over and over again in parlors on Sunday afternoons, at bingo games, and at the general store.

In the spring of 1947 I took my first breath of Spring Grove's musky bottom-land air and began a journey down the path that would eventually bring me back to tell the common stories lived out along the banks of the Nippersink Creek.

Republican Picnic

*M*y father's family were all Democrats. My grandparents were from German peasant stock, farmers who came to the Midwest for its rich, black, prairie soil and for its scarcity of Teutonic feudal lords. Most of the twelve children that my grandpa and grandma May raised spent at least a part of their lives farming, usually on small spreads that they rented from absentee owners. My mom and dad were tenants on seven different farms within the space of twenty-one years.

Dad said he liked Democrats because they were for "the little guy." Some of the German Americans in McHenry County left the Democratic party during World War I when Woodrow Wilson declared war on Germany. My father was spared this conversion, perhaps because the war didn't touch his life significantly; he didn't serve because of a rheumatic heart, and years later he would credit a Democrat, FDR, for getting the country out of the Depression.

My mother's family were businesspeople and they were Republicans. Her father owned the general store in Spring Grove during the 1920s and '30s, and her sister Eva ran the store after my grandfather died. My Uncle Paul opened a Chevy garage just up the street from the store. Other businesses in town included Shirley's candy store (which featured a soda fountain and restaurant), Walt and Terry's farm store, and Joe Brown's tavern.

Each business was known by the name of its proprietor, for familiarity was the order of the day. Walt and Terry sold Allis Chalmers tractors, but their shop was always "Walt and Terry's." Uncle Paul sold Chevrolets at his garage, but it was "Paul's garage." And no one ever said, "I'll meet you at the candy store"; they met you at just plain "Shirley's." Few people shopped in other towns, choosing instead to bargain with friends.

Though Spring Grove was isolated from much of the outside world, there was of course the intrusion of the two world wars, the Great Depression, and in my day, the Russian Threat; discussions of these concerns helped to pass the time. About two-thirds of the political discussions in town took place at my grandfather's store and at Uncle Paul's garage. The other third of the rantings were divided among the folks at Walt and Terry's, Shirley's, and Joe Brown's.

My father was less likely to argue politics than to tell a joke, a story, or some funny thing that had happened to him. But talk of taxes, foreign policy, farm subsidies, and the like was relished by my Uncle Paul. He had only gone as far as trade school but was probably the most well-read man in town. When I was in high school, I stayed with him when his wife, my Aunt Alice, was in the hospital. Their small Victorian bedroom, with its dark woodwork and papered walls, was crowded with magazines in scattered stacks on the floor. Some of these piles were about as high as their old bird's-eye maple dresser, and most of them contained bookmarks or were opened to a particular article. At night, my uncle would grab two or three of the magazines as he walked by on his way to bed, where several more would be open on his lamp stand. Most of them were news and business magazines, but some were about airplanes, photography, and fishing, to name just a few of his many interests. (He had reluctantly abandoned his sporting in fireworks when, on a particular Fourth of July while he was serving a term as mayor, one of his rockets pierced the window of the bank and exploded in the lobby.)

It was the news of politics and world events that seemed to rile my uncle the most. I slept in one of the twin beds in his room whenever I spent the night and was privy to his advice and viewpoints concerning the world situation. He seemed genuinely distressed by public affairs, shaking his head and *tsk-tsk*ing his disapproval while he read silently.

I used to go to my uncle's garage to fix my bike and put air in the tires. He'd let me use the tools and the air pump, not paying me much attention, especially if he was arguing politics. There were times when he could barely contain his disgust and discouragement with the Democrats and with FDR in particular, though he was dead by then. My uncle believed that Roosevelt had lost China to the Communists, turned the country socialist during the Depression, and generally been a "rotten, devious, crooked SOB" with no understanding or sympathy for the small businessman, who was, according to my uncle, the backbone of the country. Uncle Paul would pace back and forth on the cement between the two grease bays, in full view of his customers but with his eyes to the floor, giving the appearance of talking very loudly to himself. On these occasions I would take my time with my bike repairs and watch the commotion.

It seemed to me that my uncle's body was all curves— no points at all, just round—as if he had smoothed everything down with all the pawing and adjusting he did to himself while carrying out these harangues. He'd abruptly drop his head into his hand, rub his face, his head, the back of his head, and his neck, all in one pronounced and earnest sweeping movement. The gesture would stretch the rubbery skin of his face into a frightening rearrangement of muscle and sinew—but only temporarily, since his skin, loose and pliable from years of handling, would quickly and obediently drop back into position.

Still pacing back and forth, he'd then pull his nose, hike up his pants, and push his lower dental plate out and in with nervous thrusts of the jaw, never losing his train of thought during this impressive display of body language out of control. I thought of his large, round, body as a piece of clay molded by his own prodding and kneading into a single soft, giant, human worry bead.

Once, Dad and I were at the garage getting our Chevy tuned and listening to Uncle Paul and Uncle Charlie complain about the Democrats getting us into wars, raising taxes, and giving too much away to the farmers. My dad listened to the discussion with only a little interest, but I thought he might finally comment since I knew he enjoyed "getting Paul's goat," as he liked to say.

"Did I ever tell you about the first Republican picnic held in Spring Grove?"

My uncles turned to Dad and waited for him to continue. He was about ten years older than they were, and they had grown accustomed to the simple pleasure of hearing past events in the community described by someone who was considered an elder and a pretty fair teller of tales.

"Yeah, it was nineteen and seven or eight, and this judge came out here on the Fourth of July. He came all the way from the county seat in Woodstock to drum up some support for the Republicans. They had all kinds of beer, fried chicken, potato salad—the precinct committeeman's wife must have made two dozen apple pies. Had everything all set up on long tables next to the creek there behind the church. Didn't cost a thing so they had a good crowd.

"After they had filled up pretty well and fired off some

smoke bombs and firecrackers, the Republican judge got up there on a hay wagon to make a speech. His audience was in a pretty good mood after the feed, and they were cheering and carrying on just about every time he opened his mouth— so much so that he was, you know, feeling kind of excited with the heartfelt show of support and all. In fact he was starting to have that rising of the blood, that stirring of the spirit that all those politicians depend upon to pull them through.

"'How many of you out there are Republicans?' he queried.

"He was starting to bellow like an old Jersey bull. As far as anybody could tell, everyone cheered and answered the question to his liking. He was pleased with the response, but just to make sure he was on the right track, he had to take it one step further.

"'There aren't any Democrats here, are there?'

"It got real quiet like it still does here in this part of the country when you ask such a question as that. The judge squinted like a schoolmarm, examining the crowd. Now there was an old farmer, I believe it was Skunk Adams's father, standing under the big bitternut hickory tree there, who answered the question. 'Judge, I guess you could call me a Democrat as far as that goes.'

"'Well, are you or not?' demanded the judge.

"'I expect that I am,' replied the old man.

"The judge straightened himself, stood tall there up on that hay wagon and shouted back, 'Now why in the world would you want to be a Democrat?'

"The old farmer jingled some change in his pocket and seemed to look thoughtfully down into the muddy creek water, taking the question to heart.

"'My father was a Democrat. His father was a Democrat, and I even heard tell that my great-grandfather was a Democrat, so I guess that makes me one too, don't it?'

"The judge paused for a moment to make sure all eyes were on him, for he knew that he had that old farmer in a pickle. He would now use all of those extra brains that he believed God gave Republicans at birth to spring a cold, cruel, bear trap of a lesson on this ignorant, old Democratic farmer.

"'No sir, it most certainly does not! There is absolutely no reason to be a Democrat just because your father was a Democrat. No reason a-tall. What if your father was a horse thief? Then what would you be?'

"Well, it got real quiet, and everyone in the crowd that day turned to the old man to see what he might answer.

"'Why then, I'd be a Republican.'"

Dad had a smirk on his face as he cast a glance at my uncles and gave me a wink. They chuckled, got off the stack of truck tires they had perched on while listening, and slapped my father on the back. My father continued, "And then that old dirt farmer smiled a rotted-tooth grin, pulled an Indian-head penny out of his pocket, and flipped it at a small boy in knickers, who watched the penny fall into the grass and then pounced on it."

Since my uncles were having these laughs at their own expense, they naturally challenged the story.

"No doubt you were there, too, huh Shorty?" my Uncle Charlie grumbled.

"Yep," said my dad, as he pulled a large, old, green coin from his pocket. "Still got it right here."

My uncles howled!

This is one of the tales that I heard my father tell many times through the years. He never tired of its frisky jabbing at the Republicans, who where the dominant political party in his native McHenry County for most of his life.

A friend of mine heard me tell it once and recalled his grandfather, a farmer in Michigan. He said his grandfather would occasionally get a little careless with his farm equipment and leave it out in the weather. When the inevitable rust and neglect took its toll and the machine wouldn't function, the grandfather would proclaim that it "had gone Democratic on him."

Having heard this all of his life, my friend's father, replying one day in school to the teacher's request for the definition of the word *Democrat,* answered in a sincere and dutiful fashion that "a Democrat was something that didn't work and was no damn good!"

Terror in the Barnyard

*I*t was a horrible thing and it lived on our farm. I wasn't old enough to go to school yet, so sometimes I'd spend all day watching for it. I'd look out the kitchen window and see it stalking around the barnyard. It had a big, bulbous, yellow eye and a red face with polyps all over it. It would spy on me from the thick grass that grew around the sheds, or it would hide in the corncrib.

Stored corn must be dried or it will spoil. Back in those days we picked the corn in whole ears so we didn't need propane dryers to draw the moisture out of the shelled corn. After we picked the corn, we dumped the ears into cribs—frame buildings with gaps between the side boards. These spaces were just narrow enough to keep the corn from falling out but were plenty wide to allow the wind to blow through.

As the corn was fed to the livestock all winter—and the following summer while the new corn grew—the pile in the crib would seem to melt and finally disappear. That's when the creature would go into the crib and hide. It would watch for me through the gaps between the boards. I would some-times see it, that awful yellow eye watching for me. Whenever I saw that eye, I'd run back into the house.

I think every one of our neighbors had some animal on their farm that would terrorize the children. Sometimes it was a cranky rooster that was clearly the head of his flock but acted as though somewhere in the narrow space between its beady eyes, deep within the recesses of its flat head, were the brains and analytical know-how to govern every aspect of daily farm life, including the activities of the humans. Its means of enforcing its bird-brained decrees was to run head-long at the object of its ire, jump up in the air with wings flapping and spurred feet slashing and scratching, land on the ground, jab with its sharp beak, and then jump straight up again. This was a particularly frightening encounter if one was about three feet tall and the vertical leap of a demonic chanticleer brought its crazed chicken-face to eye level.

Or the rogue in question might be a billy goat, with thick, curved horns. Now if you lived on a farm with an evil billy, one with mischief and cunning in its heart, you had to calculate the exact location of the goat relative to your own position at all times, especially if you had plans to bend over sometime during the day. If you lost track of the goat or, even worse, forgot about it altogether as you reached down to pick some rhubarb or asparagus, the goat was liable to culminate a pretty deadly running start against the south end of your north-bent gardening operation, inflicting a good deal of pain, to say nothing of the aggravation. Whole families on some farms would be the brunt of such a beast. My dad and I would stop to visit and ask, "How ya doin'?" They'd reply, "Oh, pretty well," as they limped around stiffly, going about their business, stealing an occasional look over their shoulders at the goat, who would be grazing innocently in the orchard, looking every bit the docile family pet.

Well, on our farm it was not a rooster or a billy goat. It was an ornery, cantankerous, vile, mean-spirited Muscovy duck. Wild in the jungles from Mexico to Brazil, these ducks are now domesticated for their succulent meat by farmers all over the world, and frankly, the ducks are unhappy about it.

Barrel-chested and angry, they have the pugilistic attitude of web-footed prize fighters. They are big, heavy ducks that can't fly, but they can really move on the ground. They attack by running down their victims and beating them with their wings. My dad used to say that if one of those wings hit you just right it could break your arm, especially if you were six years old and little like me.

Well, I was six years old and little like me. The duck was just about my size. When it stretched its long neck straight up in the air, it could look me right in the face. It was a very scary thing, looking right into the face of a jungle duck. I could usually tell when the duck was about to attack. It would stand very still, with its neck stretched straight up to see. Its head would be cocked to one side surveying everything with that yellow eye. Its glaring face was all red and covered with nodules. When I saw its head in this position I knew that it was thinking mean duck thoughts.

Sure enough, in the very next instant the duck would stretch its neck out parallel to the ground and charge, its bill open wide, emitting a hissing sound, neck swaying from side to side, wings flapping wildly. If I spied this beast from the safety of the house, I just stayed inside.

One day I looked through the kitchen window out onto the barnyard. It was clear. No duck. Then I checked the corncrib and the long grass. No duck. So I opened the kitchen door that led out onto the porch, walked through the doorway, across the porch, and down the steps. I surveyed the yard. No duck. I ran across the yard to the barn and stopped to rest up against the side of the building. I looked both ways. No duck. I flattened myself against the side of the barn and carefully made my way to the door that was on one end. I stopped and looked over my shoulder. No duck. Unbeknownst to me, the big Muscovy was waddling along the other side of the barn just around the corner, so that when I got to the door, there it was. We both stopped and gazed at each other momentarily, eyeball to eyeball. Duck!

I turned and ran to the house as fast as I could go, but the duck was right behind me, flapping it wings. Its neck was stretched out so that its gaping bill was about over my shoulder. I could hear it hissing in my ear. Every once in a while, the wings would brush up against my back and send shivers up my spine that I can still feel today whenever I'm in the presence of potentially violent birds.

At last I reached the front porch. I leapt onto it, opened the door, and hurled myself into the kitchen, slamming the door behind me. I had made it. I hated that duck!

One day, my friend Donny Austin came over to visit. I was always glad to have visitors because living out in the country can get kind of lonely. My nearest friends were girls my age, and though I liked visiting them, it was special to have a boy come over now and then. Donny was our land-lord's nephew, and he lived in Chicago. He was older than me but he didn't know anything about farms, so we were on relatively balanced social footing. We hitched up my Welsh pony, Patsy, to the pony cart. The pony cart was a little bit fancy. It was a red buckboard with a high bench seat, a wagon bed, and yellow wooden-spoked wheels. Donny sat next to me on the seat while I handled the lines, steering the pony. We drove all around the farm that day. We went out into the pasture and stopped by the creek to look for frogs and kildeer nests. Then we drove up into the woods and ate some sandwiches that my mother had made for us and packed into a paper bag. She had also made lemonade with real lemons and poured it into a large fruit jar that we kept under the bench seat within easy reach.

Since Donny was from the city and didn't know anything about farms, I took it upon myself to educate him. For instance, sometimes we'd park the pony cart and run down hills. As every young person knows, this can be an adventure on an especially steep hill because the pull of gravity is sometimes greater than the ability of the legs to move fast enough to keep the body upright. The challenge is to keep from falling and rolling to the bottom, which is actually not such a bad result if you are performing this manuever in a city park where the grass is thick and the terrain kept smooth and free of rocks so that the groundskeeper can easily mow it.

On a farm, the situation is altogether different. If you trip running down the hill, there are any number of dangers to encounter, including rocks, thistles, and the dreaded cow pies, otherwise known as prairie wafers, or cow chips. If you go into a roll, it is impossible to control speed and direction. You just hope that no cows have been grazing on that particular hillside lately or, if they have, that the sun has had time to come out and dry the crust of the little bovine land mine in order to minimize the damaging stains and odor. A fresh pie is kind of a cross between a green meringue and an alfalfa puree. These can be so deadly as to completely halt the day's activities and send the unfortunate victim back to mother and the farmhouse for a bath and a fresh change of clothes, as well as a verbal thrashing from the busy farm wife.

After Donny and I had finished our lunch and resumed our ride in the pony cart, a cock pheasant flushed right in front of Patsy. The pheasant rose quickly into the air amidst a raucous cackling and a beating of wings that caused adrenaline to surge through our bodies. Unfortunately, the pony felt that same jolt of terror, perhaps magnified many times since the bird's tailfeathers brushed right up against her nose. She took off at a dead run, the cart jostling along behind her with Donny and me inside. I pulled as hard as I could on the lines, but Patsy either had the bit between her teeth or was so scared that she didn't even notice the piece of steel pulling hard against the back of her mouth.

We went through the creek and across a flat meadow and were heading directly into the woods. Thinking we would hit a tree, Donny panicked. He stood up and was about to jump off, when I remembered that my dad had said to keep a runaway horse moving in circles. I pulled hard on one of the lines. Patsy responded to this and in a surprisingly short time I had her turning in the meadow, making smaller and smaller circles until she finally was down to a trot and then a walk. She stopped, her sides heaving, soaking wet. Donny was shaking even more than I was, and I realized how scary animals can be, particularly to someone raised in the city.

Donny was certain I had saved his life. So impressed was he that for the rest of the afternoon he was very attentive to my instruction on the farm flora and fauna.

"Hey Donny, look over there!"

"Far out!" he replied.

"That's a cow, yes sir! See that, Donny?"

"Wow!" Once again, awestruck.

"That, Donny, is a chicken, damned right." Sometimes when my friends came over, I liked to use some of the swear words that I had learned from Dad's horse-trading friends or from my mother.

Well, we had quite a time that day, what with the runaway pony, playing on the hills, and me pointing out all the interesting farm animals. It was about dark when we headed back to the house, hoping we weren't in trouble for missing supper. It was just twilight as we pulled the pony cart back into the barnyard. Everything was gray—the sheds, the house, and the sky—except for a thin purple line behind the barn where the sun had just set.

That's when I saw it. Something that stood out from the grayness, a white form. It was the duck! It was in the grass next to the toolshed, waiting for us. Its head was held high and still at the end of his outstretched neck. It was watching us with that yellow eye. Then it made its move, lowering its head and spreading its wings. As it charged, its wings began to flap and that ugly head began to sway back and forth. It pointed its red face at Donny and me, and across the yard it came.

Now, I wasn't real afraid because Donny and I were on top of the pony cart. But I thought that the duck might spook Patsy like the pheasant had. Since I didn't think I had the strength to stop another runaway, I figured I better get Patsy out of the duck's line of attack. I turned her and gave a little "getty up." Her change in speed and direction must have thrown that duck's aim off, because the next thing I heard was a *thump!* I had hit the duck with the front wheel of the pony cart. I pulled Patsy to a stop, set the hand brake, and I jumped down onto the ground to see what had happened. Donny stayed on the cart. The forward motion of the cart caused the rear wheel to come to rest on the duck's neck, which was pinned against the ground. It wings were flailing up against the wooden spokes of the big yellow wheel, and its mouth was slowly opening and closing, opening and closing.

As I looked down at it, something inside of me just did not want to rescue that duck. But the moment of indecision passed. I said, "Donny, come down here and grab that side of the wheel and I'll get this side." Slowly we lifted the heavy wheel, but it was too late. The wings gave one last, noisy flourish, the gaping mouth stretched wide open, gave a start and froze, and that yellow eye turned a blue-gray as its neck went limp. The duck was dead.

We unharnessed Patsy and let her out to the pasture. Donny and I rolled the cart into the shed. We got two shovels and went back to bury the duck. But when we got there the old drake was gone. There was a wagon track in the dust running right over a pile of feathers, but no duck. There were no dog or fox tracks, nothing to show where the body had been dragged off. There were no duck tracks, either, and those big farm ducks couldn't fly. It had just flat disappeared!

That's when Donny said it. He looked across that pile of bloody duck feathers and said, "The ghost of the duck is loose on this farm. And it's goin' to get you!"

And I said, "Naaa."

And he said, "Quaaaaack, quaaaaack!" as he held his arms up over his head, his fingers scratching the air, his eyeballs bulging in mock terror.

And I said, "Naaa."

And he said, "Quaaaaack, quaaaaack!"

And I said, "Shut up, Donny!"

He was scaring me, and I was glad when he was called to dinner at his uncle's house down the road. But then I had to sleep alone in my room that night—except I couldn't sleep. I kept on thinking about the duck. I hadn't told my parents what happened, hadn't gotten it off of my chest because I was ashamed. Even though nobody on our farm liked the duck, every farm animal is valuable, and I felt like I had let the family down. Mostly what was on my mind was that I had never killed anything before.

I'm sure that I had been awake more than half the night, at least, when I heard a sound, a noise in the hallway outside my bedroom door. At first it was like a scraping, but as it got closer to the door I could make out a kind of whispering, rasping sound that I recognized immediately. It was the sound I had heard the duck make as it beat its wings up against the wooden spokes of the pony cart, the sound that the duck had made in the throes of its death. I got out of bed and walked to my bedroom door. I felt a chill. Now this was summer, the middle of haying season, but the room was cold. As I was about to grab the doorknob, I saw frost forming on the wooden panels of the door. I called out for my parents.

No answer. I called again. I knew they must be home. Nothing.

Now, I really didn't want to know what was on the other side of that door, but I didn't want to be trapped like a rat in my room either. I looked back at the door. A thin layer of ice had formed on it and there was a mist coming through the keyhole. I grabbed the door and slowly opened it.

There it stood: the old Muscovy drake. I recognized him immediately because his neck was broken and his head was dangling upside-down alongside his neck and his mouth was opening and closing and the eye was all yellow again and looking right at me as if to say, "You did it. You did it." Then he opened his bill grotesquely wide and a horrible sound came into the room. It started soft and high like a dying rabbit, but then it got louder and fuller until it was almost a roar, and then became a deep cavernous bellow like the sound made by one of our bulls—the one we had to sell because it got so mean and dangerous.

And then ... "QUACK! QUACK! QUACK! QUACK!"—raucous and unbelievably, ear-splittingly loud—"QUACK! QUACK! QUACK!"

I had a sensation of spinning through the air, weightless, white lights flashing all around me and then a sense of dissolving, first my arms and legs and then the rest of my body, until I was finally just a small gray dot sinking into the bedsheets. Then gradually I began to feel my body again, growing out of that small, fuzzy dot in the reverse order of my dissolving, fingers and toes, hands and feet, arms and legs, and then an awareness that I was in my bed once again. I sat up in bed and looked at the door. It was closed. The room was empty and quiet. I could see a little bit of lemon yellow mist in the gauze curtains on the window.

Morning, I thought, with that sense of complete relief and redemption that comes when one escapes a nightmare.

Lying back down on the pillow, I thought of something that assured me that it had all been a dream. I remembered that Muscovy ducks don't quack. Instead, they hiss and peep. It's a characteristic of their breed. Relieved and squirmingly happy, I dug myself a little hole in the mattress, buried my head in the pillow, and settled into a luxurious early-morning sleep.

That's when I heard it—a peeping noise coming from outside my window. I pinched myself and gave my head a couple of hard, brain-rattling shakes. The sound was still there. I got out of bed and walked over to the window. I leaned on the sill and looked through the screen. I saw the duck. It was standing right down there next to the bushes, digging into the mud and grass with its beak. Its neck was a little dented, but its head was right where it belonged. Every once in a while it would look up at me with that yellow eye, but I didn't care; for the first time in my life I was glad to see it. It meant that I was not a murderer after all.

From that day on, everyone in my family called our Muscovy "The Spectral Duck," or "Poultrygeist." I wasn't so afraid of the duck after that, and it didn't bother me much, either. My dad said he figured that the duck probably wouldn't trouble me again because I was such a pain in the neck, and then he chuckled.

Christmas Eve
in the Barn

On the farm we always decorated our tree just a day or two before Christmas Eve. Most of my friends in town had theirs sparkling for days and thought we were odd. We, in turn, thought they were citified and too anxious to buy things. Ours would always be a balsam fir, usually kind of thin and misshapen, looking as if it needed a friend, just like those trees in the fairy tales that were not pretty or happy until they were decorated by a family with lots of children and lit up all bright on some dark night in a small house on a wide prairie. Dad used to say that the cost of trees was "way out of line," so he'd find one that was missing a branch here or there, and priced to sell. The main thing was that it *smelled* like Christmas—that balsam fragrance that was all warm spice and wildness. The balsam tree is called old-fashioned now. It wasn't then. It was the only Christmas tree we knew, and it's the only one that seems like Christmas to me still.

Before I was old enough to do farm chores, I stayed in

the house when it was cold. The days before Christmas Eve would find me helping my mother cut out gingerbread cookies, licking the tasty frosting out of various mixing bowls, and generally sampling all of the Christmas sweets. I'd sprinkle the anise cookies with little green and red candies out of a shaker and put silver-balled faces on the gingerbread men.

At long last, Christmas Eve would arrive. Mom had been baking feverishly for days, and the smell of anise and ginger was heavy on the drafty air of the old wooden-framed farmhouse. The eve of the great day was what counted: Midnight Mass, lighting the tree, the gift exchange, Santa's arrival, the holiness of the cold night sky—out in the country away from the town lights, the deep dark of the heavens made our stars the brightest. Christmas day was for visiting relatives and getting a few token presents. The night before Christmas was the real celebration.

Each Christmas Eve I would be sent to the barn while my dad did the milking, forced to leave the warmth and cheer of that old farmhouse for the pungent cold of the barn where the only warmth was the steam rising from the huge bodies of our friendly milking Holsteins. It had to be done. There would be no Santa unless I was sent to the barn. The consolation, of course, would be the presents stacked under the tree when we returned to the house. We'd open them before going to Midnight Mass.

The barn did not have its usual appeal on those long-past Christmas Eves of white snow and dark sky. On any other occasion the barn was a hotbed of real and pretend adventures. There were the hay twine tug-of-wars with Sport, our collie, and my squirting aim to be perfected. For I was just learning to draw a weak trickle of milk from my cow, Midnight, while I watched with admiration as Dad expertly squirted milk from a big Holstein's teat right into the mouth of one of the cats sitting on the lime-covered, concrete apron. On Christmas Eve I had no interest in climbing up the chute into the hayloft to crouch on top of hay bales and wait to pounce upon evil, unsuspecting outlaws, my imaginary horse Trigger cleverly hidden in the milkhouse.

No, on those Christmas Eves in the barn I stayed close to the heavy, wooden, double doors. By leaning my entire weight against the planks of one door, I could nudge it on its rusty track. From there I was able to see the sky and the house. From there I could watch for Santa. I guess if I had seen the sleigh and reindeer descend from that star-packed black sky I wouldn't have been so much surprised as afraid that I would spoil the evening's magic by catching Santa in the act. Would he and his team bound back into the dark sky upon seeing my nose and one eye jammed between the great doors, watching?

On one particular Christmas Eve—I was probably five years old—Dad finished milking thirty or forty cows in what seemed to me like slow motion. He finished washing the pails in the milkhouse, flipped off the lightswitch, and walked toward the big doors where I kept my annual vigil. We walked outside. As Dad pulled the doors closed, we turned to the lights of the house, leaving the cows to their mangers—two farmers coming home to Christmas.

This was one time that I didn't have any trouble walking as fast as my dad. The snow squeaked under our feet in little bursts. Then we heard it. Just a quick *thump* barely distinguishable from the sound of a calf bumping the side of its wooden pen, but different enough to make Dad and me stop in unison. The snow quieted under our boots. On cold windless winter nights sounds carry in a way that makes everything seem immediate and close. The noise scared me so that I turned around more quickly than my father, just in time to see a shadow at the window in the haymow.

I gave a little gasp and pointed to the window, but the

shadow was gone before my father could see it. "Something's in the haymow."

Dad spoke softly, like he was too busy wondering what it was to expend much energy talking. "Probably a raccoon. They can make a mess in the grain bin."

He turned back to the house, quickening his steps. I ran behind him. As we walked under the yard light our shadows caught up, sprinted alongside, and then passed us. Dad opened the door and walked into the shanty room outside the kitchen, where we hung coats and left our boots and coveralls after working in the barn. Instead of taking off his boots, he turned to the narrow cabinet next to the kitchen door. He opened the cabinet door and took out a long, canvas sheath that held his .410 shotgun. My father mostly used the gun to scare off chicken-killing foxes or possums. Sometimes my older brother would take it squirrel hunting. Dad loaded the gun with three narrow, red shells that had shiny brass caps, and put a couple in his front shirt pocket.

"Jimmy, you stay here."

"I want to go! Please!" I begged. This was adventure— real grown-up stuff. I had even forgotten about Christmas.

"All right, but you stay behind me, close behind me."

We walked back out across the yard, our shadows slower but more determined than before as we passed under the yellow spray of the yard light. The snow bore witness to our excursion with tracks and squeaks.

When Dad opened the barn door and flipped the light switch, the cows all turned toward us, surprised. Some of them mooed a greeting.

We climbed the short ladder to the haymow. Dad was careful to reach high over his head and lay the gun up ahead of him on the hay before he pulled himself up the ladder with both hands. He treated the gun with an uneasiness and respect that frightened me. Hay bales were stacked all around us—green, rectangular boulders, some of them piled to the rafters. We didn't see any raccoons. The smell of the clover and alfalfa reminded me that the haymow was my favorite place on the farm. Dad stalked over toward the grain bin. He took a slow step or two as he stretched his neck to see through the doorway of the small enclosed room that was about half-filled with oats, and then he froze. From behind him I saw it too, shadows flickering on the wall of the bin.

"Fire!" The word leapt from his throat. There are few terrors to a farmer like the fear of a barn burning down, the damage to hay, grain, and livestock sometimes more than a family can survive. We ran into the bin empty-handed except for the useless shotgun. We had no hose or water buckets. I suppose we thought we could stomp the fire out with our feet.

But the fire was not out of control or threatening the beams and hay. There was only a candle, stuck to an old gray plank, with a man huddled over it. He was rubbing his hands like he was washing them, warming them over the clear flame, which seemed perfectly still in the cold air. His clothes were piled in layers on top of him so that he didn't seem to have a shape at all.

"What the hell!" Dad burst out, surprised but seeming relieved that the barn was not burning down. The stranger let out a low scream and sprang to his feet with startling quickness.

"Don't shoot! For cripe's sake, I'm just tryin' to warm up, get some rest."

My Dad looked puzzled and then glanced down at the gun, which he had forgotten about. He tightened his grip on it. "Why are ya in my barn?" he asked.

"The train," the man said as he leaned a little against the barn wall and caught his breath. He spoke quietly, squeezing his words out one at a time with a whisper-tail at the end of each. He was about as old as my father but worn-out look-ing. I felt a little sad that we had scared him so badly. "It pulled up on the sidetrack over in the farm supplies yard. I couldn't sleep there, too cold. I saw the barn and figured the cows here would keep it warmer than the boxcar."

"Where are you going?" I asked him. I'd seen hobos riding the train and sometimes walking the tracks. I always imagined that they were going to Chicago or maybe out west. He looked surprised by the question. He stared at me for a long while like he was mad, then his face relaxed.

"Home," he said, and then repeated it again, almost so low that I couldn't hear. "Home." He sat back down on the blanket that he'd laid out on top of the oats.

When he sat down in the light of the candle I noticed that his face was scarred and dirty and bruised purple—like the faces of other hobos I had seen. Dad said it was the dust and cinders working into the skin of these men who rode the rails. His face looked dry and itchy. I wondered when he had last laid his head upon something soft. I thought that once he got home someone in his family could help him with his face, maybe put some lotion on it. He looked cold. He was bare-headed and his hair was thin but long, down below his collar.

"I've been lookin' for work," he said. "Up and down this track all the way to St. Paul, but it's scarce." My father took his cap off and scratched his head, all with the same hand.

"Wish I could take on a man, but there's just not that much work to be done this time of the year." I knew that my father didn't have much money because he had been talking at night around the supper table about how the milk price was down and how none of our neighbors had much money either. He mentioned that he had read in the newspaper that even Santa Claus was hard up for money and that we shouldn't be getting our hopes too high for Christmas.

"Oh, that's all right, I just wanted to get a little warm here tonight, then I'll be goin', gotta get home by Christmas

Day or my family'll be worried. I got a boy just about your little fella's age. Yeah, I gotta get to Chicago Christmas Day. Train will be through here in the morning."

"We're going into the house for supper. You want to come in to eat?" I offered.

"No, I just need to get some rest here." I looked at the dirty cotton sack that was lying next to his blanket and saw a few tin cans.

"Well, suit yourself," Dad said, "but there's plenty to eat in the house."

Dad and I walked back to the chute. He turned halfway back toward the stranger. "Be careful with that candle."

I held the shotgun while Dad climbed the ladder down to the milking level. The weight of the gun and the smell of the oil used to clean it made me think of my brother and his stories of going out to hunt. My father's call from below woke me out of the daydream. I handed him the .410 and scooted down the ladder. I followed Dad into the milkhouse where large cans of milk were stored in a tank of cool water. He took the empty fruit jar that we used for drinking water and filled it up with some of the fresh milk that we had just drawn from the cows. Dad used a ladle to pour the white, frothy liquid into the jar. He handed it to me. "Take him this. I'll wait down here for you."

I climbed slowly back into the loft, balancing the milk in one hand, pulling myself up the ladder with the other. I didn't switch on the light in the haymow. I could follow the candlelight to the grain bin, and I was walking so slow that my eyes had time to adjust. I saw him before he saw me. He was sitting there in the candlelight tenderly picking at something on his face. I stepped on a squeaky board and he looked up toward me.

"My Dad told me to give you this," I said, hurrying my pace a little. I entered the bin and handed him the milk.

I saw an opened can of beans next to the candle. As he

was taking a long drink of the milk I could see that his chapped and cinder-scarred face was pocked with scabs and cuts in the dry skin.

"That milk's pretty good. I used to get fresh milk all the time when I was a boy like you."

I was surprised to hear him talk like that. I couldn't imagine him as a boy.

"We lived in town, but everybody had a cow in the back shed for a little milk. I used to do all the milking. I wanted to be a farmer when I was your age. Nowadays you got to go to the store for everything. Yessir, this fresh milk is swell." He took another drink, tipping the jar all the way up and finishing it. Little foamy rivers of milk ran out each side of his mouth and down his blue, whiskered chin.

"Jimmy, it's time to go in," I heard my Dad calling.

"If you want some more just go down to the milk-house."

He nodded. "Thanks," he said, and handed me the jar.

I climbed back down where Dad was waiting. We turned the lights off again and walked to the house.

"Do you think he'll get home by Christmas?" I asked my dad.

"I imagine he will if he jumps an early train tomorrow."

This time we walked straight into the house, where Christmas had erupted everywhere. The tree was lit up and there were some toys and packages underneath. I ran into the living room, dropped to my knees, and slid across the floor. By the time I stopped I was under the Christmas tree. I looked up and there it was, just about at eye level, the cap I had asked Santa for. It was plaid, bright red and black, just like the one the boy hunters wore in my older brother's collection of adventure books. I wore it all night while I opened my other presents and watched the rest of the family open theirs.

My best toy present was a plastic model horse. It was a

brown and white pinto, its neck arched and its right leg raised
in a high prance. I loved the horse and named him Paint. I
got a couple of shirts and some Tinkertoys that looked like
they'd be fun, but I couldn't make any of the things that were
shown in the pictures on the outside of the box. We all
showed each other our presents, and then my sister Diane
put some Christmas carols on the record player. Bing
Crosby sang "White Christmas" and "Winter Wonderland."
My dad sang along, and it made me think of his stories about
riding in cutters and bobsleds when he was a young man. I
thought it was a fine Christmas Eve.

We sat close to each other, grateful for the tree and the
presents and for what seemed the impossible beauty that had
descended upon that cozy wallpapered living room filled
with colored light and warm smells. We had supper right
away after the Christmas carols. All during supper I thought
of the stranger in the hayloft and his canned food. After we
ate I asked my mom if I could take him some of our supper.
I figured she'd let me because of her great-uncle Matt who
had been in the California Gold Rush of 1849. He hadn't
found any gold but he found out what it meant to almost
starve to death and to rely on handouts to survive. He had
told my grandmother never to let anyone go hungry, and my
grandmother had told my mother. She looked curiously at
my dad. I guess he hadn't mentioned the man yet.

"He rode a train onto the sidetrack today and was
looking for a place to get warm. I think it's all right if he
sleeps in the haymow. A man should have a real bed on
Christmas Eve, I suppose, but we don't know anything
about him," Dad said.

"Well, I'll fix him some food anyway." Mom began
packing up some leftovers from our usual Christmas Eve
supper of smoked herring, potato salad, and homemade
dinner rolls. She put it all into a cardboard shoebox.

"Can I take the food to him?" I said. My mother looked

at my father.

"You've got to get ready to go to church. You better let me do it." My father hadn't gone to Midnight Mass since my brother got his driver's license. He said it was too late to stay up and then milk the cows in the morning. There was never any getting away from milking the cows, even in the coldest winter on the biggest holiday. I liked it better when Dad went to the late mass with us. When we got home from church, he would fix us hot milk before we went to bed. We'd light the tree up again and sit in the living room. That's when he'd tell us about going to dances in sleighs.

"Can I go with you? I can climb up the ladder and I'll come right back down real fast to get ready for church." I figured Dad didn't like climbing that ladder any more than he had to. I was right.

"Okay, but let's get going." He stood up from the table. I jumped off my chair and grabbed the shoebox. I ran it out to the shanty porch, where I put on my coat and boots. We walked outside again. The night was even darker.

"Do you think Santa gave anything to the guy in the barn?" I asked my dad as I gazed skyward.

"No, I think Santa's got about enough work just taking care of all the children."

"Do you think he'll get presents when he gets home to his family? Do you think Santa brought something for his little boy?"

"I s'pose, but why are you so worried about it? Your mother says you worry too much."

"I just wondered," I said.

I knew it was getting colder because the snow was even squeakier and my dad was carrying an old army blanket that we kept on the porch for laying out on the grass in the summer.

Just about all the cows mooed when we opened the doors this time. They seemed to be getting used to our coming and going. After I climbed the ladder to the hayloft, Dad handed up the blanket and the box of food. I followed the glow from the candle into the grain bin. He had the candle in a tall, empty coffee can now. I could see that he didn't want to burn our barn down. He didn't hear me coming this time. I figured he must be a little hard of hearing like our milkman who had been in the army artillery during the war and said he was near deaf in one ear and couldn't hear very well out the other.

I walked slowly, afraid that I'd scare him again. The stranger was opening one of his tins with a pocketknife. He was stooped over the small shiny can, eyes fixed intently, his thick, cracked fingers worked the small blade in a tight, jagged circle, steadily, patiently, like he was familiar with the difficulty of this simple task. His face seemed older than Santa's had at the dime store, and his bruised skin seemed to shine through the stubby white whiskers. In fact his whole face glistened. Then I saw it in his lap—an empty jar of Vaseline jelly. He had rubbed it into the cracks and cinder wounds of his cheeks and then his forehead and chin. The jar was empty. I was glad he had put something on that sore face.

I coughed a little, and he jumped again. "Jesus Christ! you scared me." I said a short prayer like the priest had said to do when I heard the Lord's name taken in vain. (Sometimes it was all I could do to keep up with the prayers and the cussing when we visited some of my dad's horse-trading friends.) He saw me looking at the jar.

"Keeps your skin warm," he said. "Weather like this, you need to know every trick there is."

"My mom and dad said to give you these." I handed him the box and the blanket. He got that look on his face like he had when he told me he was going home. He took the blanket first and set it down. Then he reached for the warm box of food. He took it slowly, silently, almost the way that our missionary priest, Father Plesa, picked up the communion chalice at retreat masses. My mother said that Father Plesa was the most reverent priest she had ever known. The old man laid the shoebox down carefully on his blanket. He took the lid off and sat back on his haunches. He still hadn't spoken.

"I can bring you something better tomorrow, turkey and mashed potatoes and yams, pumpkin pie. We can't have a fancy meal tonight because it's a fast day and we're going to Midnight Mass."

I didn't need to say anymore because about then he grabbed a piece of smoked fish in one hand, a dinner roll in the other, and stuffed them both into his mouth. He chewed fast and hard, his chin moving up and down furiously. He made me think that I might like eating in the barn, too, not having to use a knife and fork or worry where the crumbs might land.

"I got to go now and get ready for church. This blanket will keep you warm. It's wool. It's always itchy when we lay on it in the summers out on the lawn. That's how I know it's really wool." He nodded.

I ran back to the ladder and climbed down. Dad was throwing some silage into the manger of one of the cows.

"You'd better hurry or your mother will be mad." I ran out the doors and all the way back to the house as fast as I could. I didn't want to be late, and I didn't like being alone in the dark. By the time I reached the house I was all puffing and my face felt frosty, but my head was nice and warm because I had on my new, red hunting cap with the earflaps down.

The church bells were ringing by the time we walked up the steps and into the vestibule of St. Peter's. It was nearly midnight but the whole town seemed alive, the sidewalks full of people. That it was so late at night seemed to make the Christmas Mass even more important. There were red ribbons fastened to each of the pews and tall Christmas trees in the sanctuary at the front of the church. We sat pretty close to the front because the people who had come early got the seats in back and in the middle. I liked sitting up front, though; I could get a good look at the statues depicting the nativity scene underneath the evergreens. These figurines of the Baby Jesus, Mary, Joseph, and the angels all seemed to have divine, beatific facial expressions. Even the cows and donkey looked like saints, which made me think that animals must go to heaven. The church was full of good smells from the fir trees and incense.

Father's sermon was about how God had chosen a humble manger among animals for His Son's birthplace. Father said that if Christ had been born now, He probably would have chosen a barn. I thought about the stranger in the haymow. While others were celebrating Christmas in their houses, in churches, and at parties, he was the one that was in a barn, just like the Christ child. Then Father talked about the story of the Good Samaritan who helped a stranger who had been beaten and robbed and left to die by the side of the road. The Samaritan bound up the stranger's wounds and took him to a place of lodging where he could recover. I thought about the tramp in our barn, and I hoped he would be home this Christmas Day so that someone could take care of him.

When we got home, my dad was still awake. He said the tramp had kept him up, that just as Dad was about to get into bed he noticed the lights on downstairs in the milk barn. When he got into the barn, he said, the tramp was walking up and down the aisle, talking about how he was going to own cows someday when he got back to his family. Dad said it took a while to get the old fellow to go back up and get some sleep; he couldn't figure whether the tramp was dreaming or sleepwalking or if he had a bottle of whiskey or wine stuffed somewhere. Dad said the only thing he could smell on the man was smoked fish.

My father made some warm milk and some onion sandwiches. These sandwiches were his favorite late-night snack. Everyone else went to bed, but I stayed up and told him about the Good Samaritan story. Dad said it was a good story and that farm people took a story like that to heart and that I should always remember it, but that I also should be careful around strangers and never get into a car with one or anything like that. I said that I wouldn't.

Before I was down to the bottom of my cup I asked Dad to tell me about his father, my Grandpa Pete, taking the whole family to church in the bobsled. Dad said that sled was the only thing to use when there was snow on the ground because it held all twelve children and Grandma and Grandpa. He said on the way home all his brothers and sisters would fall asleep but he'd sit up on the seat with Grandpa. He said when the snow was deep you'd hear nothing but the muffled sound of the horses' hooves and once in a while a distinct sleigh bell from someone else riding home on the latest church night of the year.

I had eaten my sandwich by the time Dad had those horses home from church. I figured that I missed a lot not being alive when you could take a sleigh to church, but I felt lucky to have my own pony and a father who could tell me the story. I told him that I thought these were the sweetest onions we had ever had; then I must have fallen asleep because the next thing I knew Dad was bending over my bed and kissing me good night.

I woke up early on Christmas morning. I got dressed in a hurry and then went straight for the hand cream. My mother never used it. I had thought it would be a good idea for Mother's Day instead of the red geraniums that Dad and I usually got each year at the Wilmot Greenhouse. I had seen the cream in the Raleigh man's box of wares when he made one of his regular stops. He said it was really a body cream and the company was trying it out to see if the farm women would like it. It was called Lilacs in Paris. My mother, who was particular about such things, said it smelled more like a plain old American dog had lifted its leg on the lilacs, and she tried to throw it out. I convinced her to keep it for my father's sake, but we went back to geraniums on Mother's Day after that. I personally thought it smelled all right, and even Mom said it felt soothing on her skin. I carried the hand cream into the living room, grabbed one of the boxes from under the tree, and put the lavender jar into it.

I snuck around the edge of the kitchen while my mother basted the turkey in the oven. I put my coat and hat on in the shanty and burst into the cold clear air. By the time I got to the barn I had the box stuffed under my coat, so Dad didn't see what I was up to—or perhaps chose not to comment—as I waddled along, puff-bellied, to the ladder. It was a chore getting up into the mow since I was a little weighed down and not climbing with my usual ease.

It was still real quiet in the hayloft and I could see that there was no candle burning. At first I thought I was too late, that he had caught his train. Then I heard a terrible, frightening noise, like the call of a wild animal or the sound that steers make when they're being butchered. I would have just run away except that I was getting used to strange things happening in the hayloft. I heard the sound again but it was not as loud, kind of muffled, and then it came again. This time it seemed familiar, like the sound that my father made some nights when his snoring would keep the rest of the family up. In the bin I saw the pile of blankets slowly pulsing up and down in time to the tramp's raspy and irregular breaths. Despite the commotion, he seemed to be in a deep and restful sleep. His bare and slightly balding head stuck out of the mound of covers like some weather-beaten turtle's.

I wondered if his father used to put him to bed, too. I

wondered what dreams or hopes his father might have had for him. I didn't want to wake him up, so I left the box and climbed back down the ladder.

It seemed to be getting colder all the time, so I left the barn and ran as fast as I could through the freezing air. When I got back to the house, the smell of turkey was oozing out of the walls and furniture and I got myself a hot bath. Christmas Day was fun with all the cousins around. After dinner we made a snow fort, and we stuffed ourselves with leftovers at suppertime. I fell asleep on the floor before all the relatives left. That night, when Dad put me to bed, he said that he had seen the tramp get on a train about ten o'clock that morning.

I slept late the morning after Christmas. By the time I woke up, Dad had already milked the cows and finished his breakfast. He and Mom were at the table when I walked into the kitchen. It was cloudy outside and looked to me like the Christmas season had ended with a sudden gray thud.

My parents invited me to sit down at the table. My mother was smiling just a little, my dad a little more.

"I saw one of the train brakemen this morning," my dad said. "He gave me this for you." Dad reached alongside his chair and held up a brown paper bag. I couldn't understand what a railroad man whom I didn't know would be giving me, especially with Christmas over. I looked in the bag. It was my pinto stallion. I was happy to have it back, but then I thought about that little boy, the tramp's son. I looked up at Dad.

"The brakeman said he saw our friend jump a train heading north to St. Paul. The brakeman said the old fella's a regular, doesn't have a family or a permanent address."

I looked down at the horse.

"Said he'd never seen the tramp so happy before, though, unusually tickled for a man alone on Christmas Day." Dad rattled the brown bag a little with his hand so that

I looked back up at him.

"The brakeman said some of the other hobos were teasing him about how good he smelled, like he had been soaking all night in lilac water. And he also had the warmest headgear on the train, a new red cap with warm, felt ear-flaps."

I looked down at the horse again and my face was starting to feel hot. I was especially afraid to look at my mother, who worked extra hours at the typewriter factory so that we could have nice clothes.

"I figured those things were mine," I said weakly.

"It's okay," said my mom. "I guess I'll just have to get used to having a Good Samaritan around the house."

I breathed a sigh of relief and figured that the Good Samaritan had done me a good turn, too, since I had my stallion back and hadn't gotten in trouble. After breakfast I picked up the bag and ran back into my room to play with the horse. I sat down on my bed and shook the pinto out of the bag. A jagged piece of shoebox fell out. It smelled like smoked fish. The heavy black marks printed on the cardboard looked as though they had been made by some kind of wide, soft pencil. I took the cardboard into the kitchen to show my parents. My mother read the words to me, and then she put the note away in her closet with her prayerbooks and candles.

At Christmastime in later years, I would take the note out of the closet and read the words to myself:

Fer Gimmy the kid in the whit barn tanks for the cap is the bess one i iver haf in a lon time the crem feels soo goot kep da hors.

Too Much Bull

One afternoon in May when chores were done, Dad and I took a drive. I had the day off from first grade and liked car rides with my father even better than recess. Although spring is usually busy on a farm, it had rained for a week straight and Dad was waiting for the ground to dry out so that he could get back into the fields. He figured one more good drying day would get him on schedule.

We were headed for Henry Martin's place. Dad was curious to see how Henry was doing with his crops since he farmed up on the prairie where the ground was a little higher and better drained. Henry was also one of the last farmers to work his fields with horses. He only farmed eighty acres. Henry would be in his fields plowing early in the spring when it was too muddy for tractors, and he'd usually still be planting when the fields of other farmers already had sprouted yellow-green whispers of corn rows in the warm black ground. Like a turtle among hares, Henry just kept at it.

He was a small, wiry man, all knuckles, knees, and

elbows, with a quick, devilish sense of humor, which was another reason we enjoyed visiting him. He didn't have much machinery, so everything around his place seemed slower. We were also partial to Maude and Mike, his team of black Percheron horses. They were huge but friendly and approachable, unlike a lot of Shetland ponies I had been around. I could even put some oats in the palm of my small hand and feed them. They'd nibble up all of the tiny oat grains with their enormous, rubbery lips, never touching me with their teeth. Henry's Percherons were just about my favorite neighbors.

They nickered at Dad and me when we walked into their barn on that spring day. Each of the big draft horses was in its stall grinding loudly on oats and occasionally emitting a snort or stomping sharply on the concrete floor. The only other sound was the chirping of sparrows. Dad looked into each stall, studying the animals one at a time. One of the workhorses turned to look at him. Dad stood to the side and patted the broad, high rump of the amiable giant. Once he had made the big horse aware of his presence, he entered the stall and slowly walked alongside the animal, patting its flank, then the tight, muscled shoulders, working his way up to its neck—"good boy, good fellow." Dad finished his visit with a couple of quick pats on the neck and a rub of its forehead.

Dad always took his time around animals, especially horses and mules. My Aunt Mayme tells about when Dad was a bachelor farmer on his first place. He and a friend, John Retterah, were in partnership, renting the Carey farm northeast of town. Dad had bought a pair of mules that he liked pretty well. He thought they were nice and fat and "had a pretty good shine."

According to the story, his partner John was out in the field trying to cut hay with the new team and was having an awful time of it. The mules got balky on him and wouldn't move, no matter how much he cussed and whipped them.

John was known for having quite a temper, and after haranguing those mules for a good bit of time, he threw the lines on the ground and walked all the way back to the house. Dad was cutting burdocks in the horse pasture when he noticed him walking into the yard without the mules. John was in a stew. He chided Dad for buying a pair of stubborn, worthless mules that wouldn't work.

Dad didn't say much. He wasn't much to argue, according to Aunt Mayme. Instead, he walked, unhurried, to the hayfield. When he got there, he patted all around on the mules' necks and rumps, talked to them a little, picked up the lines, and said, "Getty up." Those mules leaned right into that harness and broke into a nice, even pull.

That day in Henry's barn, Dad took a long look at the team and said, "I wonder why he's not working 'em? They haven't even broken a sweat today." We looked everywhere for Henry—in the barn, the toolshed, behind the corncrib. We had about given up and were heading back to the car when we heard shouting and hollering from the field behind the barn. Dad figured we better have a look.

It was something to see. There was Henry behind that barn plowing with a Holstein bull. He had the old thick-necked, walleyed, ring-in-the-nose, slobbering fellow pulling the plow just like a workhorse. My dad watched intently, shaking his head. They were moving away from us down the row, and from our position we could see that the furrow was all crooked and that Henry was walking behind the sit-down plow, first pulling this way, then that way on the lines, attempting to correct the staggered row that was being dug in the ground. Every once in a while the bull would just stop altogether, bellow, and paw at the ground. This would prompt Henry to loop the lines around the plow seat, run around to the bull's head, grab the rope that hung from a ring in the bull's nose, and give it a couple of yanks. This would get the bull so mad that he would throw his head from side to side and bellow even louder, but at least he would start moving again. When they got to the end of the row, Henry grabbed the bull's ring rope again to turn him back, headed the other way. Finally the great beast dragged the little farmer and his contraption along the fence line to where Dad and I stood watching.

"Whoa, you big bag of orneriness!" shouted Henry as he yanked hard on the leather lines, his small body leaning back. The bull stopped. No one spoke for a moment.

Then Henry turned his head and nodded to Dad. "Shorty." (This gesture was less a greeting than acknowledgment of our presence.)

Quiet again. Only the bull moved, flinging its tail back and forth across its hind quarters, scattering the loudly buzzing flies.

Then Henry pointed at me with his chin, "I see you got your partner with you today."

"Yep," said my dad, "he'd just get in trouble at home."

The silence resumed as the flies once again took over the conversation. Finally my dad asked, "Henry, why the heck are you plowing with that bull?"

Henry took his wide-brimmed straw hat off with one hand and pulled a blue calico kerchief out of his pocket with the other. He wiped his brow, snuck a quick squint up at the sun, and then looked at Dad. "Because I want to."

"Well, it doesn't make any sense," my dad said. "You've got a good team of horses in the barn doin' nothin', and you're liable to ruin your bull."

Henry waited to speak for a few moments, like the wry, barnyard trickster that he sometimes could be, and replied, "I just wanted to show the damned fool that there was more to life than romance and tearing down fences!"

He grabbed the lines, slapped them against the bull's rump, and off they went.

The Age of Reason

I stood there in the barn on the cold concrete, looking between the dirty, whitewashed boards of the calf pen. The calf was lying on its side like it always did when it slept, but now two of its black legs stuck straight out into midair.

We lived on the Pete Nelson farm then, near the town of Richmond, about four miles northwest of Spring Grove. I was four years old or so. I liked that farm because the train tracks were near and I got to watch the last of the steam engines belching smoke as they passed our otherwise quiet place. I also loved the long driveway with its lilac bushes, and the orchard of apple, pear, and cherry trees. The barn was old, but the roof didn't leak. It wasn't a big barn, but Dad said that it held about as many cows as he could milk at his age. I used to hide when Mr. Pete Nelson came to visit, though. He was very old and never spoke to me or my sisters. He walked with two canes and didn't say much, even to my father. Dad said he was about as good or bad as the next landlord—"better than a kick in the hinder with a frozen boot," one of Dad's favorite sayings.

"Elsie died."

I heard my father say the words quietly to my mother at the breakfast table while I was in the bathroom. I finished, buckled up the snaps on my overalls, and walked into the kitchen. I climbed up onto the chair and began picking at my oatmeal.

"What's wrong with Elsie?" I put my spoon down and waited for an answer.

"She's bad, real sick. She'll have to go away." My father didn't look up from his plate.

"She's dead," my mother said. "She was sick yesterday, now she's dead."

I climbed down from my chair and ran to the closet where my heavy, wool, hooded coat hung on a low peg under my parents' and sisters' coats. I put on my boots and buckled the steel clamps just halfway up.

"Jim, where are ya going?" Dad asked me as I came back into the room bundled and determined.

"To play in the barn." I ran out onto the porch. I could hear my mother say something as I closed the door but I wasn't sure what.

The wind roared in my ears as I ran to the barn. When I got to the big, double plank doors I stopped to rest. It was sunny out, and I stood there awhile, leaning my back against the door. The sun was bright on my face, and when I closed my eyes I thought I could see the blood in my eyelids. The barn wood felt warm on my back. Then I remembered my mother yelling at me for getting the powdery white paint all over my coat, so I stood up straight, soaked up a little more sun, and then pushed one of the big doors with my hands. It didn't budge. I thought maybe it was frozen. I pushed again, and there was a little release. I leaned my shoulder and entire weight into it, dusty paint or no, and it slid open enough for me to slip in.

There's nothing as cold and damp as an empty barn in

the winter when the cows are outside. On cloudy, windy days we'd keep the cows in all day, and of course always at milking time. The bodies of the Holsteins warmed the air—a moist, friendly heat, and the cows would all call to one another and to me. I'd run the length of the barn, back and forth, bringing them handfuls of feed and scratching their noses.

I shivered as I walked the wide concrete apron that ran down the middle of the barn and separated the two rows of milking stanchions. The calf pen was at the opposite end and I took my time getting there. It was quiet in the barn. I could hear my heart, the blood in my ears, and my breath, nothing else. Usually I'd hear Elsie before I saw her, chewing or rustling the straw bedding as she turned toward the sound of the opening door. I suspected that Elsie wouldn't be making any noise, but I wasn't sure what "dead" meant. I wasn't prepared for the complete stillness of the calf's body lying there on the straw, all stretched out and frozen. She looked heavy and thick. The objects around her—the straw, the feed in the trough, her water bucket—all seemed captured in the frozen stillness that had settled upon this once frisky animal and stolen her spirit.

I knew she had been sick. I had been sick, too, with the chicken pox. But I had gotten well. I looked around at the empty barn, at the dusty cobwebs filled with the carcasses of summer flies, at the dirty windows, and I knew my calf was not going to get well, ever.

That afternoon, a large truck with a big steel box mounted on its bed pulled into our yard. A tall, dirty man with greasy coveralls got out of the truck and walked into the barn with my father and me. He tied a rope around Elsie's legs and dragged her backwards out of the pen and down the concrete apron toward the doors. She slid along, wooden-like, her big eyes blank and cloudy like the glass shooter marbles we played with in the spring. He gave her one last yank, pulled her out the barn door, and dropped the rope. She was still again. The tall man climbed into the truck, backed it up to the calf, and began to race the engine. The steel box rose. It tipped higher until the tailgate almost touched her.

A spool of tightly wound cable on the high end of the box unwound slowly, releasing a hook that slid down the truck bed with the steel cable growing slowly behind it. The driver let up on the throttle, stepped out of the truck, and came around to the back, where he wrapped the cable around Elsie's torso. He climbed back into the truck and the engine began to scream again as he poured the gas to it. As the cable wound onto the spool, Elsie began to move almost as if she were alive but more robotlike, with her legs and body assuming strange, impossible positions and angles. When her body was completely onto the steel bed, it turned on its back with all four legs in the air as the truck box began to lower to its original position. Finally, I couldn't see her anymore.

The truck rolled out of the driveway and turned west on the cement road, crossed the railroad tracks, and seemed to melt slowly down a five-mile stretch of straight, flat highway. I watched the truck all the way. My parents were both right. Elsie was gone.

I'm not sure when it was that I connected the calf's death with the eventual death of everything and everyone I knew, when it was that I realized Elsie's dying was not a freakish mistake or oddity but was the way the world worked, the way things were supposed to be. I was certain of a change in my life, like a cold, metal sensation coming over me and sucking a certain amount of my breath away when I thought about the calf.

Thoughts of death caused me to notice things that I had not noticed before, to see how this inevitable web affected others in my world. For instance, my mother agonized about having to go to the hospital for an operation. I could sense in the tone of her voice and the shape of her face just a touch of that frozen stillness that I had seen in the calf pen. I knew my mother was afraid of never coming back again, just like Elsie. I'd watch my father and see that he had a slower, more deliberate way of walking than did some of the other farmers. They had more hair than he did, too, and seemed less careful in their movements, faster at their shoveling, bucking of hay bales, and wrestling of calves and colts. I realized that my parents were old, especially my dad. This worried me, even though Elsie had been so young when she died.

Like an approaching storm that stills the air and makes the flies bite in earnest, this new awareness of my own mortality demanded that I pay attention to it. It bothered me so much that the present moments seemed unimportant. I had not yet learned to live with death, had not made the necessary and eventual adjustments that all surviving people make, had not yet found a place to submerge this knowledge so that life could be lived. Instinctively I knew that I would have to make some kind of peace with my mortality because every farm harbors death as an equal partner, a dark presence with its own essential role in the business, its own steady job. I thought of myself as a farmer but I had not yet accepted this force, and so it remained a mysterious terror.

Things didn't get any better for a while. Not long after Elsie died, one of our fox terriers was run over by a train. The railroad tracks formed the west border of the Pete Nelson farm. Our days were punctuated by the rapid chugging and plaintive call of the steam engines, and sometimes by the high, clear, metallic roaring of the whistles on the new diesels, announcing their presence to the railroad crossing at the cement road just west of our driveway as they bore down with their tons of rumbling steel.

I was standing on the hay wagon next to the barn trying to help some neighbors unload hay when Dad came up to the wagon and told me to climb down. He looked sheepish, and I knew from the pounding in my chest that something bad had happened. Dad said he had seen Dottie cross the track well ahead of the train, but then she got scared and tried to run back over the tracks toward home. After he told me I sat down on a hay bale and thought about the little dog with the delicate ears that stood straight up from her head. They were tan on the inside and black on the side that I scratched for her. She had a little, soft, bright pink tongue that I would let her lick my face with when Dad wasn't looking. Thinking of our little dog crushed by one of those huge, iron, smoke-belching trains made me understand that the world contained an impersonal danger against which being little, or young, or sweet was no defense.

A short time after my dog was killed, one of the steam engines hit a man driving a white Kaiser. He was on his way home with a bag of groceries for his family's supper. The crossing had no lights or gates and he forgot to look—or had his radio on too loud, or was thinking about a fight he'd had with his wife, or maybe he was just tired from working every day to afford those groceries and gas for that Kaiser. I was in the yard playing with my pony when I heard the train come to a clanking and clamoring stop and then watched it standing for almost an hour just past the crossing, steam hissing and smoke wafting. It waited there on the track like some black dragon that had accidently smashed a butterfly with a casual flick of its tail and now was annoyed at the delay while the crumpled thing was cleaned off of the tracks.

I wasn't allowed to go to the accident and I didn't want to. I sat on the porch and watched the comings and goings of flashing lights on the police cars and ambulance. Our horses stood in the pasture with their heads high and their ears perked, watching the activity. Their curiosity was innocent and fearless. Death spares animals the knowledge of its pursuit.

The next morning my dad invited me to ride to town

with him. As we turned out of the driveway I looked over to the crossing. There were shiny pieces of chrome and glass lying alongside the road and potatoes, red potatoes of all sizes, in the road and on the shoulder, some not damaged at all. Something stirred in my chest and throat; I thought about the creamy mashed potatoes and the light brown gravy that my mother made for our Sunday dinners. I thought about the smell of fried chicken and about our family, my brother and sisters, all dressed in our Sunday clothes. I began to cry. I remember my chest exploding and the sound pouring out of it in distinct gushes while my face became wetter and wetter. Dad pulled to the side of the road.

"Jimmy, what's wrong?"

"I'm afraid the train will hit you," I sobbed. I was remembering, at that moment, one time when he and I were riding the tractor and stopped just in time to miss the train speeding by. Dad said he hadn't heard the whistle over the loud tractor engine.

"It's all right," he said. "We just have to always remember to be careful."

"What about Mom?" I sobbed.

"What about her?"

"She's going to have an operation!" I was becoming inconsolable, resolute in my terror.

"Your mother is going to be fine. The doctor says she needs to rest."

"But she has so much work," I protested, having heard my mother voice her hardships many times.

"You just can't worry about all of this! Just take it easy. You'll forget about the train."

"I can't!" I wished he were right, but even at that young age I had correctly understood the persistence of this gray cloud named Terror, though I had not yet envisioned the many forms that it could assume in one's life.

Dad waited until I had managed to calm down to a

steady, sniffling hiccup, pulled the car back on the road, and headed toward town.

When we got home I started crying in earnest again when I saw my mother.

"He's scared about the train and the accident," Dad told her.

"There's potatoes and g-glass all in the road. Is that man all stiff now like Elsie?" I addressed my mother, figuring she wouldn't spare me the gruesome truth. My hiccuping and tear-gushing had intensified.

"Sit down over here." My mother sat down on our worn, wine-colored, velour couch and patted the cushion next to her with the palm of her hand. I sat down. She put her arm around me and pulled me against her side. She was warm, and her fleshy arm felt reassuring. It was a bright February day, and as my mother spoke to me I watched the dust floating on the angled shafts of sunlight coming through the windows. It was all yellow and lovely.

"Everybody dies here on earth, but it's not the end of life. There is another place called heaven. After we die we will all go there. You'll meet your grandparents and you'll see everyone you loved who died before you. God is there and everyone is happy. There's no sickness and no one will have to die again, ever."

I was immediately relieved. This made perfect sense. A lot more sense than what had happened to Elsie and the man in the Kaiser. I am still amazed at the complete reassurance that I felt that day.

Spring came and my pony, Patsy, had a foal with a little soft nose and a short tail that was like a narrow curly mop, which she flicked vigorously but with little effect when a fly landed on her rump. I fed the foal carrots when she got older and brushed her downy coat whenever Patsy's maternal instincts relaxed enough for me to get close. Our neighbors, the

Schmidts, had five litters of little pigs that Dad took me to see about every day, and baby chicks and ducklings seemed to be everywhere, almost sprouting out of the ground like my mother's tulips and iris plants. The air smelled like mud as the temperature rose, and Dad regularly saddled Patsy so I could ride. The foal, which we named Ginger because of her color, would follow us.

I remember this time of my youth with a kind of warm glow. I loved the farm, especially in the spring and summer. I had the run of about three hundred acres. Dad would saddle my pony in the morning, and some days I'd ride all day, my imagination teaming me with the likes of the Lone Ranger and the Cisco Kid.

I had three imaginary friends: Sonny, Tony, and Harvey. I don't remember where they came from or how I arrived at their names. I'd create adventures for them and assign them specific roles to play. They might be lurking behind a tree or pursuing me on a horse that was almost but not quite as fast as my Welsh pony. Patsy was a rich, golden buckskin with a black mane, tail, and stockings. I began riding her when I was four and she was twenty. She lived to be thirty-six and bore thirteen foals.

My sisters tell me that they would sometimes catch me talking to an imaginary person about some scheme or, mimicking my dad, about a horse trade. I loved to listen to the men in their barns, and these conversations were fun to reenact when I was alone with large, empty chunks of time.

These blissful days were finally interrupted one Saturday morning when my mother yelled up the stairs, waking me up out of a sound sleep by declaring, "Get up, Jimmy! Mrs. MacDonald is going to be here to pick you up for catechism class. Father Fritz says you're old enough now to study for your first Holy Communion."

Civilization had caught up with me. I liked Father Fritz well enough when I would occasionally see him at church.

(I was only six years old and therefore not required to attend Sunday mass, not having yet reached the "age of reason," which was seven.) But still I was not entirely enthusiastic about the prospect of giving up portions of my pony-riding and play-acting time to these religious and educational distractions, and I could not have predicted the effect that catechism class was to have on my young life.

One gray Saturday morning, just a year or so after that sunny day when I learned of the prospects that awaited me in heaven, Sister Ignacio gathered my first Holy Communion class in the front pews of St. Peter's Church, where she informed us in no uncertain terms that getting into heaven was not guaranteed, that it depended upon whether or not we could harness our sinful natures to do God's will, and that the alternative to heavenly bliss was eternal suffering in the fires of hell.

Eve could not have experienced a more doleful transformation in spirit on the occasion of her expulsion from Eden than I did upon hearing this news regarding the Day of Judgment. I remember riding back from church that morning. Mrs. MacDonald drove me and her daughter, Mary Ellen, in their silver, bullet-shaped, '49 Ford. I watched the familiar fields and farms pass by, but they had changed. Though they were teeming with plants and animals, they seemed distant and dull, trivial when compared to the central issue of saving one's soul for eternity. Most lives experience brutal disconnections, uprootings; I felt a raw place in my chest where the wrenching had occurred.

On that morning I concluded that the only reasonable thing to do was to give up childish play and earthly distractions in order to devote my full attention to qualifying for heaven. I began to lie in bed at night and attempt to conceptualize the idea of eternity and how I might spend my time in it. How long, after all, is an eternity?

I remember Father Fritz, our parish priest, teaching us

about eternity. He said that if a sparrow were to fly around the world, again and again, dragging a ribbon along the ground, the time it would take the friction of the ribbon to wear the earth down to the size of a marble would be merely the beginning of eternity. At that age I liked to try new things every day, and the thought of something never ending had the potential of being pretty ugly, even without the part about the fire and the pain. I could see that hell could be a long, slow burn.

My ruminations included long hours of staring at fires on camping trips, not because of the usual fascination with this elemental force but because of my horrific curiosity as to what it might be like to live for all eternity in the midst of flames a million times hotter than these little cooking fires. Anyone who has been burned by a match, or touched a hot oil stove, or taken a big swig of hot chocolate and known the instant, excruciating pain of even these brief encounters with the fire god would have to give the notion of hell some serious thought. I was no exception. My every encounter with heat, fire, and flame strengthened my resolve to avoid hell at all costs.

I knew that if you died with a mortal (serious) sin on your soul you went to hell immediately. Since any sin was an offense against God, they all seemed serious to me and I figured that I was in pretty big trouble. Now in the Catholic Church of my day, well before the reforms of Vatican II, mortal sins could be forgiven in two ways. You could go to confession and tell your sins to a priest and receive absolution; or, if you could not get to a priest, you could make a "Perfect Act of Contrition." You could recite a set prayer or make up words of your own, but the critical thing about the Perfect Act of Contrition was that you tell God you were sorry for having sinned, not because you feared the damnation of hell but because it offended Him—this was the "perfect" part.

I would lie awake at night saying the formal Act of Contrition that I had learned from my prayer book, repeating the words: "…. and I regret all my sins, not because of the pain of hell or the loss of the joys of heaven"—*Nooooo! Not a bit!*—"but because they offend Thee, my God…." I would say these words over and over again, trying to purge the fear of damnation from my mind and focus on the love of God. This was not easy, even in the comfort and calm of my bedroom. I could only imagine how difficult it might be if I were to be in a car accident and need to make the Perfect Act of Contrition while lying on the highway, gasping my last few breaths as I watched my own blood drain down the gutter. Would I be able to do it right? As my young life expired, would I be able to sincerely pray, "O my God, I am heartily sorry for having offended Thee, and I regret all my sins, not because I fear the pain of hell or the loss of heaven but because they offend Thee, my Lord"?

Pretty tricky stuff, not something upon which to risk an eternity. I reasoned that under such emergency conditions I would be scared to death, so to speak, of going to hell. That while trying to concentrate on my Perfect Act of Contrition I would instead be remembering all the campfires that I'd stared at, and all the hot stoves I'd touched, and the eternal fires, and the boiling flesh, and that I'd never get to the "perfect" part—where I was more sorry for messing up my buddy-buddy relationship with the creator of the universe than I was fearful of going to hell.

Needless to say, I went to confession every Saturday. I mean, why take a chance? We moved to town shortly after that fateful day in Sister Ignacio's catechism class. The old white frame house that my parents bought was right next door to St. Peter's on Main Street, so I could visit the church whenever I felt my salvation might be in danger, and I could confess my sins at least once a week on Saturday when Father Fritz heard confessions. Sometimes I'd go two or three times a Saturday because it seemed that I would invariably forget some sins until I left the confessional and sat back down in the church pew. Once when I went back to the confessional booth for the third time, Father asked me, "Weren't you just in here? Twice?"

"Yes, Father, but I remembered another—"

"Get out of here, now! You'll make a mockery of the sacrament, which would be a mortal sin!"

"Right! I'm on my way." I sprinted out of the confessional, through the church doors, and didn't stop running for quite a ways down the sidewalk. I usually never went more than once a week after that, although once I remembered a particularly big sin and had to go back and disguise my voice. I did a particularly good Maurice Chevalier that day, I thought.

Perhaps the hardest part of this keeping-out-of-hell business was that helping to save the souls of others was even more important than saving your own soul. This was quite a responsibility, but it had its benefits. Saving a bunch of other souls gave you a big head start on saving your own, though you were not supposed to be doing it for that reason—but you always did, just a little, because of your fear of the hot coals, the boiling flesh and all. In the end you were never sure whether the good you were doing was for the right reasons. Saving souls for your own good lessened your chance of getting into heaven even if you worked at it all the time.

The best time to save other souls was on November 2, All Souls Day. There was a special church rule that said you could get a soul out of purgatory every time you went into the church to say even a short prayer. Purgatory was the place you went to after death if you had committed venial, or less serious, sins. No one was allowed into heaven unless they were completely free of sin, so purgatory was kind of a halfway house. The fires were exactly like those in hell, but it was a temporary assignment and the nuns told us that everyone there was fairly happy because they knew that someday they would go to heaven and be with God and because they knew that hell was, for them, out of the picture. A "things could always be worse" attitude seemed to prevail in purgatory. This was difficult for me to understand. I reasoned that all that pain and boiling flesh would be a fairly heavy distraction. But I guess everything's relative, even after you're dead, and it made sense that the souls in purgatory would be thinking of the future since living in the present was not a concept found anywhere in the Catholic canon.

Knowing that I could spring one of these flaming hopefuls every time I entered church and said a short prayer, I set out early on the morning of All Souls Day with plans to deliver the multitudes. A devout, pasty-faced liberator of souls, I made my short journeys back and forth: open the church door, bless myself with holy water, genuflect by a pew, sit down on the bench seat, slide onto the kneeler, clasp my hands, bow my head, and repeat, with the face of some "Poor Soul" (that's what we called the souls in purgatory) clearly in my mind, "May the souls of the faithful departed through the mercy of God rest in peace, Amen." Then I would stand up, leave the pew, genuflect in the aisle, turn to the back of church, bless myself with holy water as I left the church, return to the church steps, and start the process all over again.

I would do this over and over, beginning with relatives and friends who had died and might not have made it into heaven on the first pick. I had often been picked last for softball games and I knew how bad that felt, and I wasn't on fire at the time.

Next I would pray for the really holy dead relatives and acquaintances who were considered by everyone to be a "sure thing" to be in heaven, just in case. Then came people whom I had not known personally but who I was sure were dead and might need my help to escape their suffering.

After many hours, I would be well into the generic poor souls, people whose names I didn't even know, and it was here, among these dead strangers whose faces I could not picture, that I would begin to lose my devotional fervor. I would notice my aching knees and begin thinking of grade school friends who were out playing pick-up football and making leaf forts. But how could I decide? Should I go out and have fun while my fellow human beings, dead though they might be, cried out to me from their temporary place of suffering? Could I just ignore their pleas? Would I pass a burning building and not help everyone out—particularly if I could accomplish their liberation by merely reciting a simple, short prayer? So on the one hand there was the responsibility for the suffering of countless souls, and on the other hand, a little football titillation in the crisp autumn air. It was no contest. I was determined to rot in church if I had to.

These attacks of holiness dominated my middle years of grade school. Many of my scruffy, athletic friends had written me off as a pious idiot, when, in the nick of time, puberty entered. One day in Sister Christella's sixth-grade class I noticed that Julie Sladek, who sat across the aisle from me, seemed about as heavenly as any of my previous daydreams regarding the celestial palace. With my heart flopping around like a decapitated chicken beneath my light blue oxford uniform shirt, I wrote her a note. She wrote me one back. In an instant, my life had changed.

We both loved horses, fishing, and tackle football. I now had a wonderful, tomboyish girlfriend, and suddenly I was rescued from my preoccupation with eternal damnation. I knew from studying the lives of the martyred saints that there were many things worth dying for, but during my eleventh year I was beginning to suspect that there might be even more glorious and mysterious reasons to live. The possibilities enchanted my daydreams. Although our relationship was scrupulously chaste, I began to understand that there might be a future for me where earthly pleasures were allowed, even encouraged.

A couple of years into my puppy love I had an insight that became a turning point in my life, much the way that my mother's reassurances about heaven and Sister Ignacio's warnings about hell had been. As is true of many people when it comes to Pearl Harbor or JFK's assassination, I remember exactly where I was when it happened—walking home along Main Street in Spring Grove. Deep in thought, my head down, I remember stepping on the heavily cracked sidewalk just in front of the big sugar maples by the public school.

These magnificent trees had always sanctified that spot. By daylight, they were huge and wondrous at any time of the year. Verdant, cool, and shady in the summer, they welcomed small boys out of the hot sun. In the fall they marked one sideline boundary for our football games and served as a silent, stately audience that paid tribute to our awkward and rubber-boned loping with whispering and swayings, all the while perfuming the town's crisp autumn air with burnt and decaying leaves. At night, they became the dark and foreboding forest that had to be passed in order to get to the store or to pick up the newspaper at the corner tavern, their great arms rising to brush the gaping emptiness of the dark sky with spindly twigs that waited to ensnare some careless lad.

On certain fall days, they were so gold and yellow and red and pink that even the most desperate and cynical took in a quick breath at their appearance out of a misty October dawn. While walking under those dreamy maples one particular autumn afternoon, I realized that the world just might be a place of such beauty and joy that I did not have to spend my existence worrying about punishment—post-mortem, eternal, or otherwise. It struck me that I had a right to live—in this world, on earth—perhaps even a right to have fun. These welcome thoughts were spontaneous and unexpected, and I knew not from where they'd come. Their clarity and power were singular and transforming. I shall always be grateful for the gift of this insight, a second coming of the age of reason, which I'm certain sprang from a divine source, perhaps the tree spirits with a bit of inspiration from Cupid.

Six years later, I left Spring Grove and enrolled at the University of Illinois, leaving most of my parochial devotions behind, and it was there, surrounded by thousands of non-Catholics, that I further learned to appreciate the joy and relief offered by even a moderate dose of hedonism.

The Ten Twenty

Serving mass at St. Peter's sometimes seemed a burden, especially in the summer. With school out and that heady freedom from work and routine that only the very young are allowed to experience—and then only for a short time before the intervention of paper routes, lawn mowing jobs, and other tainted activities of commerce—an entire week of getting up early in the morning and reporting to Sister Leon seemed an intrusion.

My friends and I thought of ourselves as wild boys in the summer: free to roam the woods, to fish the Nippersink Creek, and to spend hours each day circling the ponds at the fish hatchery. Playing pick-up baseball in the afternoon on those dusty, blue-skied days quenched any need that we may have had for the organized rituals of civilization.

However, serving mass in the summer proved to be a gentle discipline with its own rewards. This wasn't the first time I learned to enjoy a regimen that I had initially disliked. Before we had moved to town, I used to herd the cows early on summer mornings. Milking had to be done early, so I'd wake up at five or six o'clock. The darkness, the temperature, and my sleepiness were all disorienting, but in a matter of minutes I'd become accustomed to the early hour and begin to marvel at the world that the new day brought: the sun, orange and liquid on the horizon; the heavy, wet smell of the mint and wildflowers; the early morning fog swirling along the ground; an explosion of birdsong from a woods as I passed by. Walking down the cow lane toward the pasture, I'd stop at the crest of the hill to watch the creek below as it sent mist into the rosy air. Sometimes I'd encounter a skunk or a horned owl finishing its nocturnal prowl. We would both freeze and watch each other like startled burglars caught in the other's house. After a few moments of intense mutual scrutiny (I would have been willing to stand still for hours), the animal would matter-of-factly amble off or fly to a more remote spot. No one who has ever experienced such a meeting ever forgets these moments of breathing the same damp air as a creature of the night.

And then there were those summer mornings serving mass. I'd walk to the church, cutting across the fresh, wet grass of our back yard. The sun was not yet high in the eastern sky, but I could feel the heat radiating off the terra-cotta bricks of the church as I skipped up the steps to the door of the boys' sacristy.

Only one or two altar boys served on weekdays in the summer. The church would be nearly empty. During mass we knelt in the sanctuary behind the priest with our backs to the silent congregation. Through the half-opened windows, the summer sounds of the town waking up blended with the low droning of the priest's Latin prayers. The sun, filtering through the yellow stained glass of the windows, cast for us a golden hue in which to pray. Its warmth cheered the wrinkled cheeks of the most regular worshippers and washed the baroque vestments of the priest in a dazzling brightness. Our white altar boys' linens appeared to have been starched in heaven. The fragrance of melting beeswax candles and Sunday's incense, still in the air, blended with the bouquet of scents drifting through the window on the first warm breezes of the new day: fresh tree sap, the sweet, ripening smell of the creek beginning to expose its muddy summer banks, roses in the convent gardens next door, and sometimes the smell of fresh-cut hay, drying out in some farmer's field. Though I knelt there on those new, soft mornings praying to a God that I could barely fathom, in Latin words that I didn't understand, the sublime commingling of ancient ritual and vernal sensations assured me that I lived in a holy place.

After mass and communion, my mother would fix toast and eggs. Then I'd be off to find my friends. The prospect of owning the rest of the day to do as I pleased seemed even more tantalizing because my freedom had been purchased by good works and a sacrament.

My friends and I spent most mornings walking around the ponds at the fish hatchery. The mornings were so crisp and filled with possibilities that we usually didn't play anything organized like baseball or hide-and-seek until we had had our fill of creeks and ponds and until the sun had risen high in the sky, its light becoming mundane, dissolving our shadows, and burning off that morning edge to the air that so excited our youthful spirits with a yearning for untamed adventure.

Our fish hatchery was the largest in the state of Illinois and brought a measure of fame to Spring Grove. The first thing we'd tell a stranger about our town was usually, "I'm from Spring Grove—largest fish hatchery in the state!" There were eight spring-fed ponds filled with the clearest water imaginable, brimming with fish, turtles, frogs, crayfish, and freshwater mussels. Weeping willows, hawthorns, and crabapple trees grew in the parkway between the ponds. The fish were hatched and raised here by the Illinois Department of Conservation, and then stocked in ponds and lakes

throughout the state. Some of the eggs were hatched in large
bottles and tanks inside the fish house, a long, single-story
brick building. We'd go inside and watch the tiny specks
emerge from little jelly-ball eggs. The fish grew in larger
tanks and finally were put outside into the ponds. The fish
hatchery occupied fifty acres south of the Nippersink Creek
to the west of Blivin Street, which ran north and south
through the middle of town. The whole area had once been
a large swamp where my father remembered cutting ice
when he was a young man.

The state had purchased the property and constructed
the ponds, each of which had its own character. What we
called the big pond was the grandest. It was a lake surrounded by weeping willows and a shoreline of rocks and
tangles that housed chipmunks, snakes, and an assortment of
other shy creatures. The middle of this pond was shallow and
formed a small, muddy island that became a haven for hundreds of turtles during the summer dry season, earning the
name Turtle Island. I used to watch the turtles through my
binoculars—they looked like little piles of black dishes bath-
ing in the sun. Years later the long-forgotten but pleasant
image of this scrambled heap of contented, yellow-eyed,
basking reptiles returned to me when I learned that certain
native peoples refer to the earth as Turtle Island.

All of the ponds except the big one were completely
surrounded by ten-inch-wide concrete walls of varying
heights. We loved to "walk the walls"—to walk on the top
of a concrete wall as far as we could without losing our
balance. This was a challenge because of the cracked and
crumbling surfaces as well as the fear and distraction posed
by the threat of falling to one side or the other—into either
deep water or the muddy slime at the bottom of a drained
pond.

The smallest pond formed a long, narrow rectangle and
was home for huge goldfish. The walls that ran its length

were the most frightening of all to walk because they were bordered on both sides by other deep ponds. Most of the ponds had walls that ran along the parkway so that if you lost your balance you could bail out by stepping or jumping down onto the grass. When you walked the walls of the goldfish pond there was no such security, nothing but deep water on both sides for the entire length.

Until we had mastered walking the goldfish pond, every other wall walk was a rehearsal for the real test. Sometimes on these practice runs the drop down to the ground might be four or five feet, but it was still better than falling into the water—most of us didn't know how to swim. The younger boys and those new in town would begin their training by walking the walls of the shallow ponds bounded by parkway. With the growth of courage and experience these apprentices would attempt deeper ponds or a wall that rose up high above the grass. Finally, there would be the goldfish pond: first on hands and knees and then standing upright, arms out to the side. The first time I made it across standing up I realized—along with the joy of accomplishment—that contrary to my parents' warning, the worst doesn't always happen when you take a risk. We walked the goldfish pond hundreds of times. It was, perhaps, a tempering of our spirit equally as important as attending mass.

As we all grew older and more sure-footed, walking the walls became less a test of stature and more a comfortable ritual to perform on our daily walks as we talked among ourselves about sports, girls, and our futures. But conquering the goldfish pond represented the passing of a milestone on those mornings bathed in yellow sun and silver water.

There were lots of things to see at the fish hatchery. We never knew what we might find on any given day, which was part of the adventure. Sometimes the giant largemouth bass—we called him Gorgo—would be feeding in the shallows of the big pond, so we'd go over to one of the smaller ponds and catch a frog to throw to the bass. The frog would land in the clear pool, be still for a moment, and then start swimming for the shore. Sometimes the big fish would ignore the frog; seeing us on the shore, he would glide into the deeper, darker water. But sometimes our offering would be accepted into that great fish's world, and the bass would turn, causing a gentle rising of the water that would buoy the frog up for a moment. An explosion of foam and bubbles would signal the amphibian's demise and then the water quieted, settling into gentle, enlarging concentric rings. We watched in awe. This was the kind of fish that could never live in our muddy creek. This was a sacred fish that needed the paradise provided by the hatchery, a fish we would never catch but could only watch and feed, and whose regal presence we could share.

We used to daydream and talk about such fish as we walked the walls. "What if they'd let us fish here for just one day? What would you do?" my cousin Vic asked.

"I'd catch a pail of frogs and fish all day for the big bass," I said.

Billy said, "I wouldn't. I'd fish in the deep pond next to the goldfish because there's trout in there."

Billy loved trout. He had adopted trout as a kind of totem animal in the way that children fix upon something to mark their identity in a world that tricks them into thinking they aren't special enough. Then again, maybe Billy simply recognized that trout, those beautiful, wild fish that refuse to live in anything but the purest, crystal water, were as good as anything to pin his hopes on. He lived with his mom and five sisters in the apartment over Shirley's candy store. He said that someday his uncle was going to take him to Wyoming to catch trout in the mountains, that his uncle worked in a factory in Woodstock and hadn't had a vacation in a while—otherwise, Billy figured, he would have probably gone to Wyoming several times already.

We were like serfs, not permitted to hunt or fish in the king's forest, but at least we could walk the walls and dream.

There was a certain pond, though nearly dried up, that was surrounded by mystery—the whale pond. It had once held deep water, but in my time it was a shallows surrounded by tall, fissured, concrete slabs. The cracks in its cement sides caused the steep walls to list in odd directions. Legend had it that a baby whale was once brought there and its thrashing had caused the walls to crack and the water to splash out over the sides of the pond. This was a rumor of considerable interest, and my friends and I pestered the conservation wardens for years until we finally got to the bottom of the tale. The real story was that Wisconsin sturgeon had once been exhibited at the hatchery, but they had been held in a much smaller tank-like facility. While sturgeon can weigh hundreds of pounds, they were not responsible for the crumbling walls of the whale pond. Although we were deflated by this shattering of our local mythology, we were still grateful that this little pond, when frozen in the wintertime, made a perfectly-dimensioned hockey rink.

If the glittering waters and flowering trees of the hatchery were the town's proudly worn jewelry, the gems that shone most brightly for me were the weeping willows that grew between the ponds and were nourished by their waters. I had never seen one until my family moved to Spring Grove, and I thought them to be the most beautiful trees in the world. Their grace and elegance satisfied me completely, and since Spring Grove's fish hatchery was the largest in the state, I figured that it must be the only place on earth lucky enough to have weeping willows. Sometimes we'd pull a single, long, spindly willow twig down to make a "buggy whip" that could really crack. If you grabbed a bunch of branches and climbed up onto a high pond wall you could swing out over the parkway and back to the wall again. The willows were the first thing to turn that springtime misty green color. The weeping willows were golden in the fall and the bare twigs remained yellow in the drab of winter. They were the long-haired maiden–sentinels of our fish hatchery.

The summer I was ten, we were having an especially hot August. I had been to the fish hatchery every morning that week and was sitting on the iron park bench in front of the store, looking for something else to occupy my time. I had just put four cents into the gumball machine, hoping to get the striped winner that could be traded for a nickel candy bar, my real desire. Though my luck was not so good, I was content to watch the cars go by while I chewed a large, purple-black wad of green, blue, red, and orange gumballs.

My cousins Vic and Dan came over, and we sat there together wondering what we were going to do that day. Dan was Vic's older brother by a year. Tall, blond, and athletic, they were older than I and could usually defeat me at any athletic endeavor, so I was grateful whenever they included me in their games and schemes.

We had already eliminated several possibilities for the day's activities. For one, we had finished scouring every ditch and roadside within bicycling distance in our quest to find discarded pop and beer bottles. This was actually a weekly job because there would usually be a new supply of bottles in the ditches after each summer weekend. It could be lucrative, too: returned pop bottles earned two cents and beer bottles as much as five cents for the quart-sized ones. Edna, who managed the store after my Aunt Eva was hired at the post office, was always glad to see us bring the bottles in, even though they meant more work for her with little profit. I think she was happy to see us being industrious and cleaning up the countryside.

It was a little too early in the morning to play baseball. The outfield grass would still be wet; besides, on hot summer days we usually kept baseball as the afternoon back-up in case we couldn't persuade any of the older teenagers with drivers' licenses to take us swimming at Twin Lakes. This kind of discussion was not unusual in our small town because one of the constant challenges was to make our own fun and we tried our best never to be without something to do. Finally, after several dead-end proposals, Danny said, "We could go watch the Ten Twenty."

I looked at him blankly. I had just lived in town for two years and it seemed that there were always things that I didn't know or had never experienced. Though most of my growing up was in Spring Grove (we moved off the farm when I was eight), I would never quite live down being the farm kid to my cousins and other Spring Grove urbanites who had lived in town all of their lives.

"The streamliner, it comes through here every day at ten-twenty in the morning. It's really fast and it rips the mailbag off the post without even stopping," Dan explained.

I looked at my big-dial Timex wristwatch that I had won selling Christmas seals for the missions. It was 9:55 A.M.

"Let's go!" I said as I picked up my bike, jumped on the pedals, and headed for the depot, my legs pumping hard. Vic and Dan caught up and then passed me on their bicycles at the bridge on Blivin, just north of the train station.

The track of the Chicago, Milwaukee & St. Paul Railroad—which we called simply the Milwaukee Road—ran through Spring Grove at the south edge of town. This rail line was Spring Grove's direct link with the city. My grandfather, Nick Weber, used to take the train into Chicago to order his general store merchandise and to shop at Marshall Field's on State Street. Wayne Brewer's father took the seven o'clock train to the city to work each day and returned with a few other periodic commuters at five-fifty. There was no reason for the Ten Twenty to stop in the middle of the morning. It just ran right on through.

I had been up to the tracks many times. In fact, walking

the rails was the next best thing to walking the walls of the fish hatchery. Sometimes we'd put pennies on the tracks for the trains to run over. We learned not to do this for the trains that did stop. A slow-moving train could make a bumping sound when it hit a penny; the conductor would hear it and give an earful to any kid who might be standing around the depot, whether he was guilty or not.

Other times, three or four of us would stand on the tracks to see how long we could stay when a non-stop was coming. We'd stand there watching the signal light alongside the track go from green to orange to red. Then the distant light of the engine would appear, faint like the glint of the sun reflecting off steel. The light would gradually brighten and grow larger. We'd feel the ground begin to tremble under our feet and then hear the whistle blow two miles away as the train sped through the crossing on Wilmot Road. As the ground would shake harder, we'd begin to sweat a little, imagining what it would be like to be stuck with maybe a foot wedged, caught in the switch track, knowing that you could never ever move from this spot, train or no train. Finally, the train would round the bend just on the other side of the Blivin Street crossing near the depot, a hundred yards away. The engine would lean into the curve like a giant, iron snake ready to uncoil and snuff out our young lives, roaring angrily as it approached the crossing. We'd scatter in all directions, laughing off our fearful curiosity and timid explorations of mortality and the limits of courage.

But I had never seen the Ten Twenty grab the mailbag, and I was glad for the prospect of this new curiosity on that dog-day morning. It was 10:00 A.M. when we rolled our bikes onto the crushed, purple, quarry stone that surrounded the depot and was used for the bed of the train tracks. As we laid our bikes in the grass next to the depot, we could hear the telegraph tapping Morse Code. The stationmaster was working alone in his small, grimy office. Most of us were Boy

Scouts and fascinated by the code—though amazed at how indecipherable the station's tapping sounded. We never asked him or any of the clerks to help us understand it. None of us knew the railroad men. They frequently changed their assignments, so there would be a new station agent every year or so; also there was for us a mystique about railroad workers similar to that of soldiers or policemen. There was something intimidating about them that we recognized even as young children. The railroad companies ruled the land in those days before the interstate highway system was completed, and the power of those companies, perhaps, gave even their workers a certain formality and prestige that separated them from the townspeople.

As we waited there for the train, an old, blue Chevy coupe pulled into the parking lot. The car door slowly swung open and old Pete May stepped out. I didn't know Pete very well. He was related to me in some way or other, but the May family is so big that mere bloodline did not guarantee that we'd think of a person as family. Pete was short with thin gray hair atop his small, round, pixie-like face. He was a retired farmer but always wore his overalls, and he had a glass eye. He was the only person in Spring Grove with a glass eye and that alone would have made him a minor celebrity, but of even greater interest was the story of how he lost his eye: it had been blown out by dynamite.

My dad had told me about it. In the early days of farming in McHenry County, dynamite was used to clear the land, to blow out tree stumps and boulders. When you dynamited you'd use two charges, a main charge and a smaller charge called a dynamite cap that ignites the larger, more powerful one. Sometimes these caps fell unnoticed to the ground in a field or woodlot, or in some cases, live caps were mistakenly discarded as defective, non-explosive duds. According to my father, Pete was digging a post hole one day and the point of his spade hit a cap that lay buried just under the surface. The explosion knocked Pete down and took his eye.

After he retired, Pete worked for my Aunt Eva at the post office, hauling the leather mail pouch up to the Ten Twenty every day and picking up the mailbag that the train delivered. We watched him open the trunk and lift out a leather bag. He carried it down the track away from the depot to a tall, slender, iron pole with wooden steps and a platform at its base. Pete climbed the steps onto the platform and fastened the leather bag to a C-shaped piece of metal that dangled the bag in midair from the top of the pole, where it awaited the speeding train. Then Pete stiffly climbed down and slowly walked over to the depot where my cousins and I stood leaning against the building.

"Hi Pete," my cousins both greeted him. Their mother, my Aunt Eva, was the postmistress now, so they knew Pete and just about everything that had to do with the mail coming and going each day.

"How are you boys today?"

"Fine, Pete. Is the train on time?" Dan asked.

"I imagine it is." Pete took out his nickel-plated pocket watch and looked at it for several moments, furrowing his brow as he thought. "Should be going through Fox Lake about now."

Fox Lake was five miles east of Spring Grove. Vic picked up a handful of stones and pinged them one at a time at the iron tracks. Dan and I walked the track, side by side, each on our own rail, up to the crossing and then back to the depot. Suddenly we all stopped and raised our chins in unison, responding to a distant wailing carried to us on the gentle morning breeze.

"Here it comes," yelled Dan. "Pete, how much will you give us to pick up the mail if the bag rips?"

Pete chuckled. "I hope we don't have to go through that again." He saw the inquisitive look on my face. "You never saw that happen did you, Jim?"

I shook my head.

"Well, you watch now. There's a special car on the train called an R.P.O., which stands for Railway Post Office, and there's a postmaster in there who sorts the mail while the train is moving. When the train comes to a depot he throws out the mail to be delivered to the town that day, then he watches for the outgoing mail from behind a little glass shield that keeps the dust and bugs out of his eyes. When he sees it hanging there on the pole, he swings a hook out and pulls it in as the train goes by. Once in a while that hook doesn't catch the bag just right and tears it open. It's a mess!"

"One time Pete paid us a quarter apiece to pick up all the letters," Vic laughed.

Pete looked at me, "I think these guys would jinx me just so they could earn the quarter!"

The whistle sounded again, much louder as the train crossed Wilmot Road. Even at that distance, the sound of the whistle bent in a way that told us the train was really moving. Vic and I walked over to the building and leaned back against it. Dan stayed on the rail.

"I dare you to stay there until it gets to the crossing," Vic challenged.

"Okay, Dan the Man will thrill the crowd and leap away at the last possible moment," Dan crowed, sticking out his chest and perching on the rail like a rooster challenging a henhouse rival.

The whistle screamed again, now just a half-mile or so from the crossing.

"Help, help, I'm stuck! Pete, help!" Dan pretended that his foot was stuck on the rail.

Pete shook his head, reached into his shirt pocket, took out a tin of Skoal snuff and pinched himself a lipful. "Kids," he muttered to himself. The whistle again, now assaulting our ears, blunt and bone-piercing, pushing out all other noise and sensation—like being in a barrel with a chainsaw.

By this time Danny was up next to the building with Vic and me, giggling nervously, his back against the silver-gray, weathered siding. We pressed our backs into the side of the depot. If you got too close to one of these speeding passenger trains, you would be sucked under the steel wheels to die a horrible and messy death. This was a "fact" known by every boy in town.

The ground was shaking violently now, as the train, big as a two-story building, sped toward us, orange and maroon bearing down. Clumps of long grass, stands of bushes, and small trees flattened and whipped up again as the big diesel rushed on, leaving a mile-long column of trembling green on each side of the tracks. As the train passed, everything rattled: the ground, the building, our own skulls and bones. The tracks and railroad ties compressed and rose in time under the weight of each axle as the cars passed. The postman in the mail car appeared before us holding a canvas bag and then seemed to vaporize before our startled eyes. Like a single still frame isolated in a movie, he flashed onto the screen of our vision for only a moment before everything reverted to blur and motion. But we knew this was no mere illusion because alongside the track we saw that canvas mailbag hit the ground, bucking and tumbling like a bronco. It finally came to rest in a thicket of grass and morning glories.

We turned our heads down and to the side to avoid the blast of air and dust, and then we looked up and to the west for the payoff, the thing we had really come to see. We kept our eyes riveted on the leather bag, squinting through the assault of the raw, sooty, diesel-fueled air in our faces. The mailbag began to rock back and forth, the pole shaking as the train passed, and then the bag disappeared; in an instant it was gone, and the train was gone! The grass swayed from side to side, slowing, quieting, until all was still and there was just a distant rumbling as the tall signal light alongside the track turned from red to orange to green.

We stood there in silence. There was nothing to say. The train had filled our lives completely, but only for a few moments, and we all felt the emptiness in its wake. Pete was a retired farmer living in town. He had spent his life working every day, growing crops and caring for animals. On the farm, his time was consumed by an unbroken strand of work with no two days ever the same. The gift bestowed by all this toil was a feeling of accomplishment, and the peace and pleasure that accompanies exhaustion. Work and life occupied the same space and there was no time to make acquaintance with the demons that inhabit idle moments. But Pete was retired now. His sons worked the land and his grandchildren lived in the old farmhouse. After his daily run to the depot, he would drop off the incoming mail at the post office and walk back to his small frame house. He'd have a modest lunch with his wife, even though he wasn't hungry, and face the long afternoon.

As for my cousins and me, now that all the excitement about the Ten Twenty was over, we knew that it would be downhill for the rest of the day. And I realized that the sight of the train grabbing the mail pouch at seventy miles per hour would never again seem so new or thrilling.

For all its grandeur, the diesel train would not define my generation or Pete's. The train would be the crowning technological achievement of his time, a generation that had worked the land with horses, but Pete would hardly ever ride on it except to go into Chicago for an occasional Cubs game or to see an eye doctor. My cousins and I would never quite belong to the train era, either; the bulk of our travel would be accomplished by car and jet plane. But for a few moments on that August morning, the two generations were united by a sense of awe and wonder at the power and majesty of that iron horse. It brought us together, and we were grateful for the moment.

When the locomotive was long gone, Pete walked over to the canvas mailbag, picked it up, heaved it over his shoulder, and walked back to his car. He threw the sack into the trunk and drove off. The three of us watched his old Chevy creep along the dirt road, stop at Blivin Street, and turn north toward the post office. We stood there quietly, holding on to the moment, and then we got on our bikes and rode slowly down the gravel road. When we reached Blivin Street, we stood up on our pedals, pumped hard on the flat blacktop, and then coasted down the hill, across the bridge, and all the way back to town.

Nightcrawlers

*M*y family didn't have many books in the house when I was growing up. We had four bookshelves, and three of them were filled with "knickknacks." On the fourth shelf was a dictionary with some beautiful color plates of birds, insects, gems, and trees, which I studied over and over; a Bible; and prayer books of various sorts— Stations of the Cross, novenas to the Blessed Virgin Mary, prayers for special occasions. We had nothing so literary as *The Lives of the Saints.*

My favorite was an entire set of *Boy Hunters,* an adventure series about teenage boys who were lost for years in the wilderness. Separated from their parents, these fierce young men survived by their wits and their hunting and fishing skills. I was captivated by these stories and always hoped for some kind of similar adventure for myself.

However, from a wilderness point of view, Spring Grove was a pretty tame place. Most of the surrounding countryside was farmland that supported domestic animals and crops but was not very well suited for wildlife. The really good hunting and fishing stories I heard were from local people who had gone "up north," which meant that they had gone to Wisconsin or, on rare occasions, Canada. We had our hunting and fishing seasons in northern Illinois, but the harvest of game and fish in McHenry County was meager. I persuaded my parents to subscribe to hunting and fishing magazines and thus retreated into an imaginary world of outdoor adventures.

In the winter, during hunting season, I'd devour all of the hunting stories in *Field and Stream* and *Outdoor Life,* completely ignoring the fishing stories. These hunting epics chronicled great journeys to remote backcountry areas: packing to the high slopes of the Rockies in search of mountain goats, treks to tropical jungles for jaguar, and sometimes the sighting of a mysterious creature, the physical descriptions of which were unlike anything previously conceived by the human imagination. When I finished the hunting articles, I'd store the magazines away somewhere and retrieve them again in the summer to read the fishing stories.

One hot summer night after supper, I was reading an article in *Field and Stream* about a twelve-pound bass caught in the Florida Everglades. I had been fishing in the Nippersink Creek all that day and had caught an undersized sunfish and a rash. The Nippersink Creek, its mud holes teeming with reptiles and other primitive creatures that sought refuge in its slimy alluvium, was one of my boyhood haunts, but a sportman's paradise it was not. About the best a person could hope for was a one- or two-pound catfish, but usually we caught bullheads.

Now a bullhead is a kind of small, yellowish green member of the catfish family. In fact it looks just like a catfish with its whiskers and beady eyes but is smaller, never weighing more than a pound; and like its whiskered cousin, it spends its life scrounging for refuse and carrion on the muddy creek bottom. I'd bring my bullhead catch home for my mother to cook for supper. She'd dip the cleaned fish in flour and pan-fry them. If they were caught in the springtime when the water was cold they didn't taste too muddy. Since the bullhead was the fish my friends and I most often caught, we considered it to be a kind of town mascot, and a fitting representation of the simple way of life in our valley—stunted bottom-feeding.

That summer evening as I sat on the porch enjoying the warm, moist air, I was filled with a longing to be whisked away to the most primitive regions of the Everglades or some other remote locale, free from the confines of civilization, where I could fish every day for my supper and hunt big game, the skin and sinew of which I would use to make clothes and shelter. My daydream was interrupted by the sound of a car pulling into our driveway.

It was Larry Elfman's light green '49 Ford—the model that looked like a rocket. Larry was a friend of my brother Paul. The doors opened and Larry, Paul, and their friend Bob Sutton got out. I was nine years old and held my brother and his friends in awe. They didn't quite live up to *Boy Hunters* standards but, to me, they were intriguing—competent vagabonds, physically powerful, always in charge of their destiny, and able to drive their cars wherever they pleased.

I watched them perform their regular parting ritual in the driveway. They sat in a row on the front fender of Larry's car, smoking cigarettes, talking, laughing, occasionally pushing or punching one another. I was particularly interested on that night because of Larry. Larry was the closest thing to a mountain man that we had in our part of the country. He hunted and fished every season; he was a trapper and could call ducks in without a duck call. He had even been "up north."

Finally, Larry slid off the fender, signaling that he was going to leave. He threw his cigarette in the grass, got back into the car, and started the engine. Bob jumped off of the fender but my brother was still sprawled on the hood, laughing and hanging onto the windshield wipers, as Larry backed down the driveway, shifted into first and squealed rubber on the blacktop, braked, squealed rubber again, and then braked to a stop.

"May, you're a maniac!" Larry shouted out the window. My brother pushed himself off the hood and landed deftly on both feet. He moved like a cat—perhaps he could have been a Boy Hunter.

"I'll see ya Wednesday night. We'll hunt some night-crawlers," Larry hollered through the open window of the Ford as he pulled away.

Bob and Paul each gave a listless wave as Larry's car noisily went through the gears down the long blacktop that led to the highway.

"Hey Jimmy, how's it goin'?" Bob gave me a wink as he and Paul crossed the porch, opened the screen door, and walked into the house. I ran to the screen.

"Paul, can I go with you Wednesday night?"

"Yeah, I guess so."

I sat down in a daze. This was too good to be true. I was going to go hunting with them. Nightcrawlers! I had never heard of such a word. Nightcrawlers? Perhaps this was it: the adventure I had prayed for, my daydreams coming true. Apparently some kind of animal, some creature, came out at night and crawled around. I thought that this must be the mythical beast of my reveries; this was the wildness that was missing from my life. I couldn't wait for Wednesday night to come.

It rained all day Wednesday, so my friends and I stayed in the house and played Monopoly. I worried that the rain would wash out my hunting trip with the big guys. I didn't care at all about getting wet, but I was afraid Paul or Larry would call it off. Much to my relief, Larry and Bob came over after supper. It was just getting dark. My brother raced down the stairs as soon as he heard Larry's car pull in. I followed

Paul out of the house and down the driveway. Larry began speaking to Paul and me as he rolled down his car window.

"This rain will really bring 'em out," he said. "I've got the stuff in the trunk."

Guns, I thought. "Can I look?"

"Yeah, I guess." Larry got out of the car and walked around to the trunk.

"I brought my own flashlight," I said, proudly clutching the chrome-encased light I had won selling *Catholic Digest* subscriptions as I followed him to the back of his car. He opened the trunk. I turned on my flashlight, which with its fresh batteries illuminated the trunk completely.

No guns! No nets! Just a flashlight and two buckets.

"That's all you brought?"

"Those buckets'll hold more worms than we've got time to catch in one night," Larry reassured me.

"Worms?"

Larry grabbed one of the buckets, took a flashlight, and walked over to our front lawn. "Yeah, the grass is loaded with 'em," he said as he waved his flashlight beam back and forth. I joined him in front of my mother's shrubbery, and it was there in that hideously genteel locale that my nightcrawler fantasy died a quiet death. For the ground was, indeed, covered with worms; it was nighttime and they were crawling.

I was, for a moment, speechless—and profoundly disappointed. I had never connected the idea of worms with the word "nightcrawler." In my fishing magazines, artificial lures and flies were the bait of choice, and I always dug "worms"—not nightcrawlers. It was at that moment that I bitterly resigned myself to the apparent reality that I must, indeed, live in the most barren of wildlife sanctums if the greatest local woodsman of my brother's generation was content to hunt worms.

But I was soon distracted from my despair by the

incredible scene that lay before me: a warm, rainy, summer's night with thousands upon thousands of worms lying in the grass. It looked like *A Midsummer Night's Dream* with all of the parts played by worms—long slippery ones, thick as my little finger, the biggest worms that I had ever seen. They seemed to luxuriate in the mist and the soft grass. Larry said they liked the rain, and when it was dry outside they'd stay underground.

Then I noticed that many of the worms were, well, "together"—coiled in very intimate pairs. As a nine-year-old altar boy, I had never seen or heard of anything like this, but I was sure that if Sister Leon found out about it, she'd be out there pulling the licentious rascals apart. But fortunately, she wasn't, so I welcomed the sex lesson, no matter the species.

I now know that the reason there were so many worm couples that night was because worms are both male and female, each worm having both sets of sex organs. (There is a scientific word for it but I don't think it's *ambidextrous*.) So being a nightcrawler means you never have to worry about getting a date. A conversation between two amorous wigglers planning a passionate rendezvous might go something like this: "Meet me under the dandelion leaves in a half hour, and if I'm not there, start without me."

It didn't take long for the word to spread, and soon a dozen of my friends and I were out on the lawn every rainy night for the rest of the summer. We were truly enthralled by the ease and sensuousness with which these slithering little earthworms went about their business in what was in more than one respect an "earthy" manner. There was none of the struggling and wrestling that I had noted in my careful observations of barnyard animals. These worm trysts on those sweet, summer nights were genuinely romantic, at least by small-town (read German Catholic) standards. So charmed were we by this idyllic display of ardor that we never caught any worms that first summer, we just watched them.

However, by the time the next summer rolled around, issues of sensuality and pleasure yielded, in a sadly predictable manner, to matters of economics.

You see, we learned that the fishermen just down the road in Grass Lake and Fox Lake were offering a penny apiece for nightcrawlers. On a good rainy night I could catch two, maybe three hundred nightcrawlers in a couple of hours. This was a lot of spending money. With that kind of ready cash a boy could live "high on the worm," so to speak, so we began to catch them.

My friends and I would cash in our nightcrawlers and head right for Shirley's soda fountain. We'd start with a giant, thirty-cent chocolate malt and then get a brown bag of penny candy to go: Mary Janes; malt balls; Hershey's Kisses; red, black, and brown licorice; Sugar Babies; candy coins; and those purple pills that were stuck to the long skinny rolls of paper. It was just about impossible to peel those little pills off with your teeth without getting a mouthful of paper, but they were a must with any big purchase. The more prudent and frugal of us would always put a little money away for requisite seasonal purchases such as kites in March, marbles in spring, exploding caps around the Fourth of July, smoking incense sticks (we called them "punks") to keep the midsummer mosquitoes away at the free movies and ball games, and of course, peashooters for the first week of school.

The very best item was a six-pack of miniature wax pop bottles filled with an artificial-fruit-flavored liquid. We'd each buy our own pack and carry it around for most of the day, drinking one every now and again. It might be three o'clock in the afternoon, and we'd have been playing pick-up baseball on the dirt field behind St. Peter's Church for a couple of hours. Those of us who had them would keep our wax bottles waiting on the benches where we could take a swig between innings. After hours of playing ball on that dusty skin infield with the sun beating down, there was nothing like grabbing one of those little wax bottles in our sweat-drenched, dirty hands, biting the top off, and pouring that sun-warmed, hot lime- or grape-flavored stuff down our parched throats—pure refreshment! When the bottle was empty we'd roll the wax into a ball, stuff it into our cheek like a major leaguer with his plug of tobacco, and be ready to "play ball" for the rest of the afternoon.

As we grew older, we could pick four or five hundred worms a night, and our spending habits reflected our new-found prosperity. We bought even more malts and sodas, ice cream bars, six-packs of real pop—and, once in a while, a new baseball or mitt. Of course, we measured the cost of all potential purchases in "worm dollars."

Although I was enjoying my affluence, there remained something about the nightcrawler business that troubled me—the dry season. June and July were the best months to gather worms because the warm, muggy air would drift up the Mississippi Valley from the Gulf of Mexico. These soft, musky winds carried the smell of the delta and brought the rain that brought the nightcrawlers. But in August the rains would stop, the lawns would dry up, and so would our business.

Naturally, the asking price for our product doubled and then tripled. The fishermen, on summer vacation in August, would pay up to thirty cents a dozen for nightcrawlers, but we didn't have any. Those who were smart had kept some money in savings for these dog days, but many of us just stayed away from Shirley's soda fountain altogether and passed the time playing ball and waiting for school to reopen.

One summer, between sixth and seventh grades, I devised a plan to hold my nightcrawlers off of the market during the rainy days when the price was low and dump them in August for thirty cents a dozen. I figured to make a killing on the nightcrawler exchange by tripling my money in worm futures.

I set about in early June to build a storage facility by sinking an old washtub in a hole that I had dug in the back yard underneath the big box elder tree next to the old chicken coop. I filled the tub with all kinds of leaves, shredded cardboard, vegetable clippings—everything that *Boy's Life* recommended for an abundant and flourishing worm farm. I found a piece of plywood for the cover, secured it with a heavy rock, and figured that I had taken my first step into market economics.

For two months straight I worked like a trooper. Every rainy night I was out there picking worms. It was a good rainy year and I was putting maybe a thousand worms a week in my tub throughout June and July. I didn't have any money but I didn't care. I'd walk uptown and look askance at my friends who were wasting their money on candy, root beer, popsicles, and peanuts. Ha! I was going to buy a new bike.

I was real proud of myself, felt like an entrepreneur, like those businessmen that I had seen handing out the I LIKE IKE buttons at the county fair. In fact, I was feeling pretty rich, even though I was temporarily out of cash—I had investments. I thought that someday, perhaps, I could be a businessman, too, maybe even a Republican. Then I could go to the Republican Golf Day without having to caddy. I imagined having a huge business. I would no longer deal with individual fishermen; rather, I would supply those big, one-stop market–baitshops in Fox Lake, the ones with signs in the window that read NIGHTCRAWLERS, REDWORMS, AND MILK.

The day finally came. It was the fifteenth of August—the Feast of the Assumption, celebrating the Blessed Virgin being assumed into heaven.

(When I was younger, I had thought that Mary had

"zoomed" into heaven. My third-grade teacher, Sister Veneranda, had straightened me out on this one. "Mr. May, the Blessed Virgin did not zoom into heaven."

"Oh, I'm sorry, Sister. She ascended into heaven."

"Wrong again. Christ, the Son of God, the second person of the Holy Trinity, ascended into heaven under his own power. Mary was assumed into heaven."

I finally got it. It was a propellant issue. Christ was God, and could go anywhere He wanted, anytime He wanted. So He blasted Himself into heaven. Mary, on the other hand, got "sucked up into heaven" by the divine forces.)

The weather had been dry for about two weeks and all available worms had been sold. I watched with satisfaction as the price for my squiggly commodity rose with each passing day. Remaining smug and resolute for as long as I could, I thought the feast day a fitting one to celebrate my bountiful worm farm by showing it off to my friends who had stopped by on their way home from church.

I led the way to the buried treasure. I figured I'd impress my friends before I sold the worms the following day. Bursting with anticipation and pride, I lifted the plywood cover off the washtub, causing about a half-dozen well-fed moles to escape in all directions, over the sides of the tub. As much as I searched, I could not find a single nightcrawler. The moles had eaten my worm herd! I had been wiped out!

I learned that day about the inherent risks of delayed gratification, and I regretted my former superior attitude toward friends from whom I would soon be begging a sip of pop or a stick of gum. Looking back, I'm not sure if the unfortunate experience caused me to be suspicious of profits gained from harvesting natural resources, or if I simply gained a respect for the more secure virtues of daily labor, but I do know that I've considered myself a Democrat ever since.

Trouble in the Grotto

Not long after that family of voracious moles climbed into my washtub and ate my worm farm, an equally frisky bunch began digging burrows next door at St. Peter's. In fact, they were doing their business in the Grotto of Our Lady of Fatima, which was the pride of the parish, the site of the annual May Queen crowning, and generally a sacred area that would have been declared off limits to furry diggers by ecclesiastical decree had any of the clerics thought of it.

It was a distressing sight to behold. There was the Blessed Virgin in all her divine splendor, standing on a cement cloud overlooking the statues of the children, their flock, and the Nippersink Creek, a scene of celestial tranquility and an inspiration to all the faithful of our muddy little valley. But alas, it was now defiled, for the little varmints were champion diggers and had constructed tunnels just under the surface of the ground, producing a maze of raised, serpentine tracks that crisscrossed among the Fatima children, the sheep, and the lava rocks. Worse still, the excavations had caused the statue of Our Lady to list decidedly and rather sacrilegiously to the east.

Naturally, the dirty business perpetrated by this unholy family of subterranean denizens caused a great stir among the parishioners, who petitioned our pastor, Father Johann Fritz, to take action. Not being a common laboring man, Father embarked upon a less direct and more spiritual strategy. He prayed—offering several masses and novenas to St. Orkin, the patron saint of moleskinners, all to no avail, bringing new meaning, perhaps, to Christ's decree that his kingdom is not of the earth.

Through all of the prayers and clamoring, the little grubbers continued to dig, scratch, and hunt worms in a most natural, if not altogether respectful, manner. Though it pained him greatly to spend the money, Father Fritz finally realized that he would have to pay someone to remove the moles, to engage them physically, *mano a mano,* in order to deliver the Blessed Virgin from this scourge.

He turned to Skunk Adams, a bachelor farmer who Father was certain would do the job for the best price. Skunk was a likable enough fellow and had many friends in town, but he had never quite found his vocation in life. He did odd jobs—cleaning wells, cutting weeds—and at one time had even served a term as thistle commissioner. He thought of himself as a carpenter, though the fellows at the lumberyard said it was a shame to give Skunk new lumber. But Skunk worked cheap, and that was enough for Father.

Father arranged a meeting in the church vestibule one day after mass.

"Skunk, I have a job for you."

"I'd be happy to give ya a hand any way I can, Father."

"Well, Skunk, as you know we have trouble in the grotto. These here moles have made a mockery of the Holy Mother. The grotto has been soiled by the wretched creatures and I want you to take care of them."

"You want me to kill the moles, Father?"

"Yes, Skunk, eventually, but don't be too quick about it. That would be too good for them. You see, these moles have committed a grievous sin, a sacrilege—a sin that mocks the Blessed Mother herself, and I can't allow it, Skunk!"

"Well, Father, I don't think it's right that you should."

"I can see you're with me on this, Skunk."

"I most surely am at your service."

"Good. Now as I have said, these creatures have sinned dreadfully but they aren't human and therefore according to canon law cannot be damned to hell for eternity, which is what they deserve. So I think the Christian thing to do, Skunk, would be to make them suffer while they're still alive!"

"It's really kind of a crusade then, isn't it, Father?"

"Skunk, you have grasped the theological and historical importance of this mission. I'm proud of you."

"Well then, Father, I best be getting at it. How do you want me to do the deed?"

"Skunk, being a priest, a man of the cloth, I am Christ's representative here on earth and also in Spring Grove, so perhaps it is better that I don't acquaint myself with the specifics of the gory deed."

"Father, I understand."

"I knew you would, Skunk."

It took Skunk a while to organize his tools, to wait for ideal weather conditions and such. But at last he was able to carry out Father Fritz's ordinance. Soon the molehills, the holes, and the raised trailways began to disappear. The grass and flowers grew undisturbed once again, and the Virgin herself was returned to her upright position presiding over her gathering of stone worshipers. The people of the parish were once again at peace and devotionally content.

It was about this time that Father Fritz summoned Skunk to the rectory for the compensation that he justly deserved. After writing him a check from the parish fund,

Father closed the checkbook, placed it in a drawer, leaned back in his chair, and looked first at Skunk and then out of the window. His gaze suggested that he was working out a moral dilemma or perhaps some ethical principal, right there on the spot.

"How did you do it, Skunk?"

"Father?"

"The moles, man, how did you kill them? You see, I need to know in order to properly record the expenditure."

"Of course, Father."

"Very well. Ah, did you lay them on the sidewalk and chop them into little pieces with a spade?"

"Oh no, Father, they did not get off that easy!"

"Oh, that's good, Skunk! Did you place them in a burlap sack and throw them in the creek there in front of the Virgin so that she could watch them die from where she is perched upon her concrete nebulosity?"

"No, Father, it was worse than that!"

"Well, that's wonderful, Skunk. Did you douse them with gasoline and light a match to them so that they could suffer the fires of hell right here on this earth, which is what they deserve for the sin against our Blessed Mother?"

"Absolutely not, Father. Much worse!"

"Well, terrific, Skunk, but what exactly did you do with them?"

"Father, I took the sinful little buggers behind the church and I buried them alive!"

Snowstorms

I'll never forget the really great snowstorms. In my
mind there have never been such storms since, although
it takes a lot more drift to be up to my neck in snow now
that I am beyond the age of making snow angels. A friend
from the tropics may wonder, *Snow angels?*

First you find a nice soft snowdrift. Then you allow
yourself to freefall backwards into this congregation of
about a billion six-sided, no-two-the-same, perfectly formed
beautiful crystals—*thwump!* (This is perhaps the best part.)
Next you do a jumping jack while flat on your back by
waving your arms and legs. A friend then pulls you straight
up and out of the snowbank so as to not mess up the image,
and there you have it—an angel with rounded wings and a
long gown outlined in the snow.

It always works; even kindergartners can nail it the first
time. Not much in life offers such perfection at so low an
investment. Such is the generosity of a snowstorm, offering
miracles and glorious sights at every turn. A really great
snowstorm transforms the world. After a night of, say, eight
inches of snow and fifty-mile-per-hour winds, the landscape

is hardly recognizable to a small child gazing out the bed-room window on a morning of canceled school.

One Sunday night in January of my fifth-grade year, I got ready for bed after the ten o'clock news. My mother and father believed that no one could have a sound reason to be up after the ten o'clock news; therefore, all decent people should be in bed by ten-thirty. It was the standard time in our family for both young and old, unless you were sick. I never volunteered the time. There are certain things children do not do, and one of those is to remind their parents that it is time to go to bed. My mother, however, would usually issue the signal. When the news anchorman would sign off, she would glance at her watch and say, "Oh my God, it's ten-thirty!" She did this every night for the eighteen years that I lived at home. At her exclamation we all got out of our chairs and up from various sprawled positions on the floor and went to bed like a herd of obedient farm animals.

We didn't have central heat, just an oil stove in the dining room downstairs. My sister's room had a grate in the floor right above the stove, so her room was always warmer than mine. My bed sheets would be ice cold when I crawled between them so I never liked going to bed in the winter, especially on Sunday nights, when there was nothing to look forward to but a cold bed and school the next morning.

The street lamp outside my window partially lit my room. It hung on a wire strung between two poles, and I could gauge the force of the wind from my bed by noticing the pattern of shadows cast by the streetlight on the wall and ceiling. That night I lay in bed absorbed in the melancholy that always afflicted me on a Sunday evening after the week-end was over and friends and relatives had left from their afternoon visits. I wanted to sleep, for if I was awake too long I would usually start thinking about all the sins I might have committed and forgotten to tell the priest at confession that Saturday, so I held my eyelids closed tightly and waited for the soft dark slumber that would always come like a faithful friend.

I'm not sure how long I did sleep that night, but I awoke to a roaring sound as the house creaked and shadows vaulted across my bedroom wall. I sprang out of bed and ran to the frosty, marbled window and looked down onto the dark street. The streetlight was tipping violently one way and then another like a bell announcing the approach of the northwest wind and its army of white. The lamp was shaking out showers of small, driven crystals visible in a spray with each peal of light from side to side.

I watched out the window awhile and then got back into bed. I was excited and hopeful but not yet smug about school being called off. There was always a chance that the snow-plows would get out before the school buses. But the plows would usually not go out unless the wind stopped; other-wise, the roads would immediately drift over again. I fell back to sleep, comforted by the stormy, conspiratorial sounds of what I hoped was a major blizzard in the making.

I woke up later to a heavy and raspy scraping that I recognized immediately as our church janitor, Matt, shovel-ing snow in front of the convent just next door to our house. Parishioners walking to eight o'clock mass had to negotiate the sidewalk past our house and also the convent. The sound of Matt shoveling was comforting on the one hand, because I knew that there must have been a considerable amount of snowfall, perhaps enough to keep the school buses from getting through. On the other hand, I felt badly about Matt. He was eighty years old, very tall and thin, and seemed to be the hardest worker in town. His face had a perpetual stubble growing over the little rosy road maps of veins on each cheek. His long slender nose was hooked and, in the winter, usually garnished by a small, clear bead of snot that had never, to anyone's knowledge, fallen off. Somehow he could shovel snow or coal, fix a radiator pipe in our classroom or move several boxes of books, all without ever losing that little bubble, which he regularly swiped with the back of his gloved hand to no permanent gain, for the enduring bead was always there, much to the glee of us schoolchildren. It was our favorite thing about Matt.

During my six years at St. Peter's School, I feared that Matt might die at any time. He walked kind of stooped over, his eyes watching the ground, and he moved with that unselfconscious shuffle common to men whose lives are so committed to and defined by physical labor that their bodies display the effects of years of damage to bone, muscle, and tendon.

When he was in his seventies, Matt painted the church steeple, setting up his own ladders and scaffolds. When the job was finally done and he climbed down, the nuns at the convent told him that they had been praying for him. Matt's reply was, "For what?"

Lying there listening to the rhythmic scrape of his shoveling, I knew that this was a job that he was content—perhaps even happy—to do. But at the same time I felt guilty—a young, strong boy like myself sleeping in my bed while this old man was out in the blizzard. I lived in fear that he would just keel over one of those mornings; die of a heart attack shoveling snow like so many people do during every Midwestern winter. Then I would have to live with the knowledge that I could have saved him by getting my sloth-ful carcass out of bed and shoveling for him on that fateful morning. Instead I would find his frozen body on the side-walk, his loyal, industrious eyes glazed over and staring up at me as I stepped over his emaciated body on my way to church, prayer book in hand, hypocritical as a Pharisee. After passing over him I would turn for one last look and notice that the little bead of snot had formed a tiny, roundish icicle. In fact, Matt lived for many years after I had grown up and left Spring Grove. Perhaps the hard work kept him alive.

I may have dozed off while listening to Matt, for I very suddenly realized that the scraping sound had stopped. I thought, "He's dead!" I sat up in bed. The room was just barely light but the wind was howling now, stronger than last night. I ran to the window. When I looked out, it hurt my eyes; it was like looking into a florescent white wall. Matt must have given up when the snow drifted back onto the sidewalk.

This looked very promising indeed, especially since my math wasn't done and I had planned on doing it at the breakfast table, which had become a habit of mine. I'd spread out my papers on the table and open the oven door to heat the room a little. My memories of doing math on those freezing mornings in the kitchen, my half-numb fingers trying to grip a dull pencil, go a long ways toward explaining why I never became an engineer.

I heard pots banging downstairs; my mother was up. I ran down the steps and swung around the corner, veritably leaping through the kitchen doorway. I was in good spirits. My father was sitting at the table. I looked at the clock, seven-thirty, another good sign! Dad should have left for work by now.

"It's really drifting out in the country," Dad said. Nestled in our little valley, we usually didn't get the brunt of the winds that pummeled English Prairie to the north and German Prairie to the south. *Drifting in the country* was the magic phrase. It meant that when you tried to drive up out of the valley the weather would get worse. The school buses could never handle the drifting. My father took off his boots and sat down to a fresh cup of coffee. "I'm gonna wait here awhile and see what happens."

I ran to the living room window. My eyes had adjusted a bit to the brightness and I could see our cedar trees in the front yard whipping back and forth violently, the outlines of their branches muted by the blowing snow. There were no car tracks in the street, in fact it was difficult to see any outline of the street at all. Our yard, the sidewalk, and the road formed one continuous white slab. I knelt on my knees with just my head over the windowsill because I hadn't dressed yet. I looked carefully at where I thought the road should be—nothing was moving, no school buses, no delivery trucks, nothing. Everyone had stayed in their warm houses, having coffee, taking their time with breakfast, listening to the radio. The town was completely shut down, frozen in its tracks. This was a big storm!

Mom called me to the table for breakfast. I ran into the kitchen. "Go upstairs and get your pants on!" She lowered her voice to a growling laugh.

While I was upstairs I heard the radio announcer. "The following schools will not be in session today: District Ten, Woodstock, St. Mary's, McHenry"—I grabbed my pants off the floor, pushed one leg in and started hopping toward the stairs—"District Forty-seven, Crystal Lake"—I stopped by the staircase and stuck my other leg in—"St. Bedes, Fox Lake." I was running down the stairs, zipping up and buckling my belt. I hit the floor running and slid into the kitchen on my stocking feet. "Lake Zurich Consolidated Schools, no school today, Wauconda High School, no school." I sat down, my arms on the table, leaning toward the radio, ignoring my food while my mom and dad ate theirs. "St. Peter's Grade School, Spring Grove, closed."

"Yeah! Hooray!" I jumped off of the chair and ran to the telephone. It was already ringing when I reached it. It was my cousin Vic; he wanted to go to Devil's Hill.

"Sure," I said, "I'll meet you there about ten o'clock." I hung up the phone, walked back to the kitchen, and sat down at the table. I was suddenly very hungry.

"You're not going out until the wind dies down," my mother said.

"Okay." I wasn't complaining. After all, school was off for the day. The weather had to clear eventually, although I remember one winter when we were off three days straight.

This time I was hoping for a clearing later in the day because I loved going to Devil's Hill. It was the best sledding hill in town.

The sky cleared about eleven o'clock. The world was transformed again, all blue and yellow in the sky with red and orange and more blue sparkling off of the sun-drenched snowbanks and icy tree limbs. We couldn't go sledding just yet. We had to drench ourselves in this white, plunge into it, surround ourselves. This was the time for making snow angels and for wading through the deepest drifts we could find.

We exploded out of our houses, dove into snowbanks, and rolled in the fluff until we were near frozen.

I returned home at noon for hot soup and a change of clothes. After I finished my lunch, I raced back out to the garage. My old sled was hanging from a nail on the wall. I saw that it needed a pull-rope so I cut a piece of clothesline with my pocketknife. I fed the rope through the holes in the steering handles and knotted it at the ends. I was ready to go. I pulled the sled across our lawn and out to the sidewalk that ran in front of our house on Main Street, then turned east and headed uptown. As I passed the houses I saw older boys shoveling driveways and sidewalks. They'd all be up at Shirley's candy store later to buy comic books and chocolate malts with the money they made shoveling. I reached into my pocket with my mittened hand to make sure I still had the dime my mom had given me so that I could get hot chocolate at Shirley's on the way home.

Some of my friends saw me passing, and soon there were a bunch of us, our sleds emerging from their long summer slumber, each being pulled from some back yard, tracks merging with other sled tracks like rivulets joining the stream as we trudged with determination, joy, and dread to Devil's Hill. We walked down the middle of the road, the snow up to our thighs. There was no traffic, no commerce. The road and the town belonged to us.

We walked through the intersection in the middle of town. The mailman was just pulling up to the post office in his jeep, and we could see a dump truck with a yellow light flashing on its roof as it pulled out of the township garage, plowing its way to the street. When we got to the edge of town we could hear the other kids before we saw them. The hill was really a steep bluff formed by the cutting action of the Nippersink. As the creek left town it meandered a little to the north and then turned back east, creating a bend on its outer bank.

This steep slope that stopped abruptly at the creek was what we called Devil's Hill. It was a short, fast run with the creek at the bottom; when the snow was hard and icy you had to turn your sled sharply at some point on the way down or roll off the sled while holding onto the pull-rope to keep body and sled from tumbling over the creek bank into the freezing, spring-fed waters. Most of us had Flyers, which were easy to steer, but some of my friends had the new aluminum saucer sleds, which were fast and virtually uncontrollable. These required a variety of athletic if not graceful maneuvers to keep out of the creek. Naturally, they were more prone to "wrecks."

The last thing we always heard from our parents before we left was: "Be careful of the creek. It's moving water. Even if there is ice on top, it's not safe." We didn't need to be warned. We had heard stories of kids who broke through the ice on the creek and were carried downstream underneath the frozen sheet. The steep, fast grade of the hill—with the creek waiting at the bottom like some icy serpent, hoping for one of us to miss our cue and be swallowed whole down into its dark muddy gullet—provided the perfect mix of thrill and dread to warm our hearts on those freezing, storm-blessed days. We threw our sleds over the fence, helped each other climb gingerly through the barbed wire, and broke at a run to the edge of the hill.

Some of my friends would not hesitate. They would flop onto their sleds on a dead run and head down the hill. I usually liked to take a look over the edge first, lie down on the sled, and then push myself into the abyss. That first run down the hill was always a sweet reunion with pleasures long fogotten over the spring and summer: the sound made by the sled runners, the cold wind and snow in our faces, and the frozen smell of the ground near our noses as we lay prone on our speeding sleds.

About halfway down the run it was important to pay attention and think about the creek bank. If the snow was wet and slow and you did not get a very good start, the sled sometimes stopped on its own before the creek. But if the hill was fast and icy you had to begin turning about three quarters of the way down the hill to avoid catapulting over the creek bank. That day the snow was deep and fluffy, welcoming me and cushioning me down the hill. I reached the bottom of the hill and rolled off the sled as I approached the creek, but the sled stopped almost immediately after I bailed out. I was still a long way from the creek. I stood up, feeling sheepish for being scared, and walked back up the hill, pulling the Flyer behind me. I went up and down the hill, again and again. It was a perfect day.

After a couple of hours, the sun began to work at the hill, melting the surface of the snow as we packed it down with the runners of our sleds and the footsteps of our rubber boots, which made prints in the snow—most showing the logo of Sears or Montgomery Ward, where our mothers bought our clothes. By three o'clock, the hill began to get icy. We didn't really notice the change at first because our speed depended upon the condition of the snow on each particular path. Maybe every third time down we'd feel runners slipping on ice.

No one saw five-year-old Danny Britz sit down in the saucer, not his older brother or sister, not the kids his own age who had come to Devil's Hill for the first time. By mid-afternoon the hill was swarming with children, so that it was hard to locate anyone in particular among the colony of brightly colored and bundled shapes scattered across the slope. But once his saucer started its descent, it attracted attention as it zipped past the runner sleds and the slower saucer jockeys.

Chance had aligned Danny's saucer with a narrow, long strip of ice that ran straight down the hill. Boy and machine were sliding with the ease of a hockey puck, smooth and fast, picking up speed like a bullet aimed at the icy Nippersink. Activity on the hill began to stop, first at the top as children turned to watch the blur that had just passed and then at the bottom where there could be heard a quiet cry, just a whine really, emitting from little Danny's throat as he careened toward the creek-bank. He went over the edge and disappeared.

We all ran to the embankment. The empty saucer was still skidding across the ice, making a hollow and lonely sound until it finally came to a stop up against the opposite bank. Brown, muddy water was lapping up out of a jagged, roundish hole and over the edge onto the ice. About the time that I felt terror welling up in my stomach, Danny stood up in the middle of the hole, screaming. He stood there straight and still, holding his soaked and freezing arms to the side of his drenched snowsuit like a wet, red-quilted penguin. He would stop screaming periodically to let out a couple of deep sobs and then start screaming again.

By now his sister and brother had found a long stick and were running to the creek bank. Danny was still standing in the icy hole. He had fallen off the saucer near the shore where it was shallow and the creek bed was fairly solid. He began calling to his brother and sister between the screams and the sobbing. They got the stick to him. He grabbed it with both hands and they pulled him toward the shore, where he scrambled up the bank onto solid ground. We all gathered around him. He stood there crying and trembling. His sister took her hooded coat off and put it around Danny. He was trembling violently and I knew from my Boy Scout first-aid manual that he was in trouble unless he got those cold, wet clothes off and his body temperature up—fast.

I remembered the "hypothermia drill" that made us all snicker and laugh when we first heard about it while studying for our merit badges. We were told that if you were out camping and someone wound up in Danny's condition, you should take off your clothes and the clothes of the victim and climb into a sleeping bag together. The warmth from your unclothed body would bring the victim's temperature back up. No one had a sleeping bag, and I don't know what would have happened if Mrs. Olson had not been home. She lived right across the street and called Doc Kagan when Danny's brother and sister brought him to the door. By suppertime Danny was warm and enjoying hot soup and cocoa.

We took a few more rides down the hill, but the creek seemed to loom more dangerous than ever. After a couple of half-hearted runs that I was careful to aim away from the creek, I walked over to the bank to look at the hole that Danny had made. The water was turning to brown slush. By three-thirty, the hill was quiet. Everyone had gone home.

Mom and Dad were still at work when we got back to my house. My friends sat around the kitchen table while I made pancakes. There's no hunger like the kind you build up on the day of a storm. My friends stood by the oil stove in the dining room, drying their pants and luxuriating in the heat. Pancakes were my specialty, the only thing I could cook real well, and it was just the thing to feed a whole bunch of cold friends. I made the steaming hot cakes in a cast-iron skillet and put lots of maple syrup on them. My friends were grateful. I liked doing it and liked that my mother trusted me to make a meal while she was at work.

After the pancakes were gone, we all sat around the table drinking milk. There wasn't much to do and nobody wanted to start dishes.

"You wanna hear a story?" I asked. I had just heard one from my older cousin Harry at his sister's wedding, and I was anxious to try it out.

"You see, there was this old lady who was real rich. She had about a million dollars and used to ride around in this big pink and black Packard convertible, all over town. Well, a truck hit her while she had her arm and elbow resting on the door of the open convertible. Cut the arm right off, and blood squirted all over the pink seats!"

My friends moaned. This was going pretty well.

"Then a policeman came and grabbed her arm but the blood was spurting all over his uniform." More shrieks and laughter. "He got her to the hospital in time and she lived. She was so rich that she had her doctor or some guy make a solid gold artificial arm. She loved this arm even better than her real one. She'd show it off to all her friends like a big piece of flashy jewelry."

At this moment my friend Roland, who was always clowning, got up and walked around the kitchen swinging his hips and waving his arm around.

"It was also good for when she didn't like someone. She could ka-bong them with it." I swung my arm around and punched my cousin Billy.

"Ow!" He thought just a moment and hit Johnny Waspi in the arm. "Pass it on, no returns." The blow darted around the table. We spent a lot of time punching each other's arms in those days.

"This rich lady loved her golden arm so much that she

had it put in her will that when she died the arm had to be in her coffin with her, still attached. She died and they buried her like that, all that gold six feet under.

"Grave robbers found out about it. You know those grave robbers, they find out about everything. They dug up her body, took the golden arm and went to a hideout back in the woods not far from the cemetery. They were in the shack and had the arm laid out on the table. They were admiring it and trying to guess how much it would weigh and how much they could buy with the gold after they melted it down. That's when they heard it, outside, shuffling around on the porch. Then a voice:'Who stole my golden arm? Who stole my golden arm?'"

I looked around the room as I said this. My friends were starting to get quiet, no horsing around. I continued with the story.

"'Who stole my golden arm?' The two grave robbers freaked out. They threw the arm in a sack, got in their car and drove fifty miles to a small, dingy motel.

"'Man, that was weird,' one of them said as he looked around the room of the motel.

"'Yeah,' said the other, 'it might have been the wind or maybe our imaginations but I'm sure glad to be out of there, away from that graveyard.'

"Then they heard it again. 'Who stole my golden arm?' It was coming from the window, through the screens. It was circling the cabin, for they could hear it as it passed each of the open windows. *'Who stole my golden arm?'*"

The kitchen had become so still that I could hear some of my friends breathing.

"They freaked out! They put the arm in a sack, ran out of the cabin, jumped into their car and took a dirt road back into the woods ...."

I paused. Looking around, I could see my friends leaning in, more interested perhaps than they wanted to be. I was setting a trap, beginning to anticipate springing it on them.

"They ran out of gas! That's when they heard it back in the woods. First it was the sound of leaves crushed underfoot. Then the sound of twigs snapping. And finally, just about the last thing they heard was the sound of fingernails on the fender and roof of their car. *'Who stole my golden arm?'*" (I looked around. My friends were ready. I was going to get them.) "*'Who stole my golden arm?'*"

Then something unexpected happened. My friend Roland stood up on top of his chair. I was ready for my surprise move and really wanted everyone still and focused, so I wasn't sure what to do. Roland raised his arms into an arc with curled finger tips like he was some kind of a ghost.

"'WHO STOLE MY GOLDEN ARM?'"

Roland now had one foot on the chair, his arms raised and the other foot in mid-air, kind of fishing around for the edge of the chair just as I sprang the trap.

I jumped out of my chair and pointed at Roland. "YOU DID!"

The effect was explosive, sort of like one of those Peanuts comic strip characters who does an instant flip surrounded by semicircular lines indicating air turbulence. Roland sailed through the air in one direction as he kicked the chair the opposite way. He slid across the floor. He hit the wall! The chair hit the opposite wall! This was even better than I had hoped. We rolled around on the floor for the next several minutes holding our stomachs and laughing.

That was the best snowstorm I can remember. It was the day that the Nippersink had shown us that death's icy gaze could sometimes blink, and we were all grateful that Danny had been spared. It was the day that I told my first really good story, a day to remember—and I do.

Sixth Commandment Blues

When I attended St. Peter's grade school, we all knew that our parish priest, Father Fritz, presided over the likes of heaven and hell. First there was the heavenly church—with its stained glass, beeswax candles that glowed halfway down the taper as if from some inner source of divine light, incense, flowers, and marble side altars that displayed icons of saints, angels, and lambs.

The church basement below contrasted sharply with its sanctified and lofty counterpart. In its unholy bowels reigned a belching, coal-stoked boiler that heated the buildings. Father always bought the cheapest soft coal stripped from the southern Illinois hills, veritably stolen from the devil's stockpile and coal-trained north to Spring Grove where the cars sat on a sidetrack while my Uncle Art and Walter Brown shoveled them empty. This coal had a high sulfur content. My mother called it dirty coal and got mad at Father every time the smoke and cinders from the chimney speckled her clean white wash as it hung on the line.

When that boiler was fired up in the winter, it made the hot water pipes clang and ring throughout the building, and the basement of the church and school smelled like something foul. We sat in our desk rows, silently toiling at our catechism, and fearing that the stench rising from the boiler room beneath the church was the breath of Beelzebub himself.

The school was an attached building added several years after the church had been completed. It grew from the rib of the grand and holy sanctuary; within its walls the children of the parish were vigorously instructed in the Catholic doctrine and ritual practiced by Father Fritz and his congregation.

In our German Catholic village, it was required that our priest be German, frugal with the proceeds from the Sunday collection, and of course, celibate. Father Fritz's pedigree on the first two counts was beyond dispute, and although the same woman served as his housekeeper for some thirty years, his adherence to the third requirement was never questioned except for an occasional joke among the farmers who composed the men's church auxiliary, the Holy Name Society, whose weekly evening meeting provided the devout farmers of the valley and surrounding prairies a place where they could escape chores, drink beer, play cards, and wear their aftershave—all after a brief business meeting, of course.

Father Fritz was not only the final authority on matters of ethics and morality; he also baptized babies, married young couples, heard confessions, buried the dead, and handed out report cards four times a year at St. Peter's School. He had been pastor at our parish for more than twenty-five years. Some said that he had lent money to families during hard times and performed other acts of charity. Perhaps he had been more engaging when he was a young man, before the responsibilities of being a local deity had taken their toll.

We called him Father, but—even though we saw him almost daily—he was more like a dour and preoccupied uncle to whom we were required to show great respect but who seemed distant, strange, and sometimes comical.

We would watch through the classroom windows as he walked from the rectory over to the church and school or on his occasional jaunts around the church grounds. He was a short, stocky man, and as he walked he rocked from side to side with his head cocked back in a regal manner, chin and cigar stub (never lit but usually well chewed) pointed upward toward the heavens, as if he were searching the firmament for spiritual ecstasy through his heavy, dark-rimmed glasses. When we met him on the sidewalk he might mumble "Hello boys"—or maybe grunt, or not seem to see us at all, as he went on his wobbly way. He was untidy and usually displayed on the front of his black cassock a good sampling of the food that he had eaten over the last few days, along with hairs from his pet Chihuahua.

His sour visage, often trimmed in unshaven stubble, was never altered by the demands of his high station. He could stand at the center of some nearly rapturous celebration of liturgy and devotion, say Easter Sunday, all surrounded by candles and incense and adorned in gold-leafed sacramental vestments—the warm glow of which improved on his usual paleness—and his countenance would remain, nevertheless, pained and unfocused.

He kept us scared most of the time by telling us that he had a paddling machine. I had never seen the paddling machine, nor did I know of anyone who had seen it or anyone who claimed to know anyone who had seen it, but we believed. After all, in the Catholic faith there were many unseen things we were required to believe in, and the paddling machine seemed a more urgent and concrete matter of faith than some of the rest.

At school we were sent out into the hall if we had

misbehaved. We were made to stand there, sometimes for hours. Several things could happen out in the hall, most of them bad, though there were some advantages to banishment from a cramped classroom of sixty or seventy children and one overworked, often angry nun. First of all, there was no work to do. Second, it was nice to look out the window. Usually looking out the window was one of those cherished luxuries to take up whenever Sister left the room. If you got caught doing it you might be reminded that it was a way to get cobwebs growing in your brain, or that idleness was the devil's workshop. Our school was set in a grove of maple and apple trees and was practically a year-round nature sanctuary with all kinds of birds, plants, and animals to watch. Finally, from the hall you could wave at friends on their way to the bathroom or sometimes even talk to them, though this was dangerous since committing an infraction while already being reprimanded was a grievous matter— sort of like an inmate killing a prison guard—and could bring on the school's form of capital punishment, namely the ruler on your backside.

Sometimes the penalty was light when you were sent to the hall. Sister would just come out and give you a good talking to, tell you how this was no way to behave and how God wanted us to learn and use our ability and not be occasions of sin for other people and stuff like that, and then you could go back to the classroom without much fuss. But sometimes it was not so easy. You might have to stand out there for hours with no way to rest your legs, until they felt all achy and weak and you'd do anything or promise anything just to be able to sit down.

One of the worst things that could happen was to be seen standing in the hall by Father Fritz when he made one of his frequent visits to the school. It was not as scary as being caught out there by Sister Leon, the eighth-grade teacher who wielded a half-inch thick ruler with relish and knew how to finish the blow with a wrist flick that Rocky Marciano would have envied. But Father Fritz had built a reputation on his use of the ruler too, especially in his younger days, and there was always the threat of the legendary paddling machine.

Fortunately, you could often tell if he was coming. The first clue would be the slamming of the heavy steel front door of the school building. This was the one closest to the rectory. It had a long bar about waist-high on the inside that opened the latch. The bar made it easy to hit the door on the run from inside the school and burst to freedom and the out-of-doors. We were always tempted to run through that door every day at the end of school, but it was not allowed. We had to walk slowly until the sidewalk ended, where explosive movements were permitted. On the last day of school, though, we were allowed to hit the door on the run. Once we were outside drinking in the fresh spring air, we would leap and dance around like ecstatic druids.

If someone was leaving the building while you were standing out in the hall, you would hear that bar click before the door slammed. But if the only sound you heard was the door slam, it meant that someone had come in. It could be Matt the janitor or one of the sisters or on rare occasions a parent, though the parents generally left the teaching and running of the school to Father and the sisters.

If it was Father, there usually was a dead giveaway: you could smell him coming. He always had an unlit cigar in his mouth that he had chewed down to about half its size. Though he never smoked it in the school building or in church, he puffed away in the rectory so that his clothes smelled strongly of cigar smoke. Now, any number of the village men smoked cigars, but Father Fritz had a unique and dominant odor, probably from the combination of the cigar, the daily ration of sacramental wine, and the Chihuahua.

Once in the door, Father would set the cigar down on

the edge of the steps that led up to the classroom level, because he didn't want the students to see him in class with it. Then he would pick it up on the way out so that he could chew it some more. His stashing of the cigar got to be common knowledge among the upper-grade boys. As soon as they knew he was in a classroom, one of them would raise his hand and ask to go to the bathroom downstairs. On his way he would stomp on the cigar. Father never mentioned what he thought about all those flat cigars, and we never asked him.

The thing to do when you got the telltale whiff was to hide. Sometimes just flattening yourself against the wall and remaining very still would suffice. Other times ducking behind a bookcase that was occasionally stored out in the hall would do the trick. With any luck, Father Fritz would amble down the hall, carefully examining the ceiling, and never realize you were there.

Unless it was report card time, Father visited the school to reinforce some religion lesson already taught by the sisters, to present some piece of religious doctrine of which he might be particularly fond, or to rant and rave at the kids whose parents had not paid their school tuition. On rare occasions he would tell a joke or story. He had one of each. The joke was, "What do you say when you see three holes in the ground?" Answer: "Well, well, well." The story was actually just a bit of biological hyperbole. He said that a rattlesnake could leap from the front of the room by Sister's desk to the cloakroom in the back all in a single bound. Of course, we believed. Since he was the priest, we assumed, he would know about rattlesnakes, and everything else.

He had a particular way of speaking during these brief lessons. The information would be laid out in concise phrases and always punctuated with "see."

"Obey your parents, see."

"Don't eat meat on Friday, see."

"Be sure to go to church on Sunday, see."

And his favorite: "Any sin against the sixth commandment is a mortal sin, see."

Here was where our ears perked up. The sixth commandment was one of the most interesting: Thou Shalt Not Commit Adultery. We knew this was an important commandment, but no one had ever explained exactly what adultery was or wasn't. We knew that adultery was some bad thing that married people could do, but the Catholic religion also included everything that might be a sexual sin under that same commandment, Thou Shalt Not Commit Adultery. It was the Catholic catchall.

So in fourth grade, Father said that any sin against the sixth commandment was a mortal sin, which meant that if you died after committing such a sin you would go straight to hell. No one told us what these sins covered but we were pretty sure that it was something dirty—not just regular dirty like when our mothers told us to be sure to wear clean socks and underwear when we played baseball in case we got hurt and the rescue squad paramedics would see us.

(I often wondered what those dedicated medical workers might in fact do or say in such a situation: "This one's got dirty socks, let him bleed to death. We're going back to the hospital. We don't have to put up with this.")

No, we were sure it wasn't that kind of dirty. When Father Fritz stood at the front of the class teaching about his favorite commandment and said, "Thou shalt not commit adultery," he'd be looking right at us fourth-grade boys. And we knew just what he was talking about. He wasn't talking about married men running off to Jamaica with their secretaries. He wasn't talking about a four o'clock rendezvous after the first shift at the Intermatic factory. He wasn't even talking about "back seat bingo" after the high school football games. He was talking to us. He was talking about the bane of every good Catholic altar boy's spiritual purity. He was

talking about the first great hurdle on the road to the pro-
verbial pearly gates of heaven. He was talking about *dirty
thoughts.*

And he was right, because we had them. All manners of
dirty thoughts, all the time. They would flash into our
consciousness—pages from the women's underwear section
of the Sears Roebuck catalogue, body parts, images of household pets copulating. They could occur at any time—in the
middle of religion class, during morning mass, while talking
with your mother.

We were very worried since these thoughts seemed
dirty enough to qualify as mortal sins. So we asked Sister
Christella. She was my favorite and was always willing to
help us with a question.

She explained that a sin was not committed until there
was an "act of the will." This was a great relief because it
meant that you wouldn't go to hell for some thought that
just flew into your head. She said that in order for there to
be a sin you had to "entertain the dirty thought." Now this
was really curious. How would one entertain a dirty
thought, exactly? You couldn't, for instance, invite one to a
party. "Hello dirty thought, come right in. Make yourself at
home. There's soda in the refrigerator."

So we asked more questions. Sister said that it had to do
with how long you held the dirty thought in your brain. She
went on to explain. If you got a dirty thought and you only
noticed it but then pushed it out of your mind, you were
guiltless. For instance, if you were doing your arithmetic at
your seat and somewhere between carrying your number to
the next column or borrowing from its neighbor, the thought
of a black lace bra from the catalog should enter your mind,
you were fine as long as you flicked the picture out of your
mind (I used to shake my head). The sequence might be:
numbers … numbers … black bra … headshake … numbers
… numbers … black bra … headshake … numbers … num-

bers. Which would be fine. But if you held the idea in your mind for a while, if the sequence was numbers ... numbers ... black bra ... black bra ... black bra ... then you'd committed a sin! It was during this time of my life that I came to understand the full meaning of the term *thought-provoking*.

The headshaking saved my soul for a number of weeks during that school year, until Sister Christella sent home a note suggesting that I be taken to a neurologist and checked for what she feared might be some kind of nervous condition that caused my head to shake uncontrollably. Well, I was nervous, yes, but I was not going to allow myself to be taken to a doctor if I could help it, so I stopped shaking. Sister said it was a miracle.

The only thing left was to go to confession faithfully to get these sins absolved from my soul. Preparing to confess these impure thoughts was a big job because it was necessary to figure out how many times the sin had been committed during the week since my previous confession. I remember kneeling in the pew outside of the confessional talking to myself. "One dirty thought every five seconds, sixty seconds in a minute, sixty minutes in an hour ...."

Finally, I'd have it calculated. I'd get out of my pew and walk into the confessional, a dark, narrow little closet-like room with a similar attached room for the priest to sit in while he listened to your sins. Confession was scary enough with any priest but especially so if, after kneeling down in the confessional, you smelled that familiar cigar.

Father Fritz would mumble something and I would begin, "Bless me, Father, for I have sinned; my last confession was one week ago. Since then I have committed adultery one hundred twenty thousand, nine hundred and sixty times"—in a town of two hundred.

It would get real quiet on the other side of the booth and then Father would ask, "How old are you?"

"I'm ten, Father."

Father was silent for a moment. "For your penance, say two Hail Marys."

I understand now that Father was motivated by genuine compassion in asking my age. At the time, however, I figured that I had set some kind of high-water mark for adulterous behavior among fourth-graders, and that I now would be exposed. However, his administration of such a light penance was reassuring, and I would leave the confessional feeling truly forgiven, a great burden lifted from my shoulders.

Agnes

On my mother's eighty-eighth birthday, I visited her at the Hillcrest Nursing Home and brought her a birthday card with words on the cover that said *A Mother Is.* The card opened to several pages, all trimmed with roses and violets, that spoke of the selfless love, the long vigils over a sick child's bed, the miracle of birth.

"I know what a mother is. I had five children," my mother said matter-of-factly, and then she laughed. As she read each verse of flowery praise she would stop at various times and say, "That's true, there's nothing in the world like a mother's love," and later, "I never thought I would have so many children. Five is a lot of children to raise; they're not having so many these days."

We sat quietly. She was seated on her bed eating the hot fudge sundae I'd brought her from Hardee's. "I've always liked ice cream," she commented. She looked out the window. The sticky wet snow that clung to the bur oak trees outside made them look like a study in pen-and-ink. Small pots of crocus and hyacinth plants rested on the sill.

"We used to ride the sleds when the snow was deep like

this. The farmers would bring their milk to town on bob-sleds, you know, the morning after a big snow. We lived just off the main street. Your Uncle Paul and I would catch the sleds just around the corner from our house and stand on the runners all the way up to the creamery, over near where the fish hatchery is now. When they stopped to unload their milk cans we'd just hop onto one of the sleds that was empty and ride it back home. It was really something, that snow!"

I reminded my mother that my friends and I used to like to grab the rear bumpers of cars after a snow and slide along behind the car on the slippery street. "Well, that was dangerous! Those cars! You could fall under a wheel. We just had sleds in those days. There wasn't so much to be scared of then."

My mother's generation has probably seen more technological change than any generation in the history of the human race. My friend, Michael Cotter, a third-generation farmer from Minnesota, told me his dad used to say, "I've ridden in an ox cart and I've ridden on a jet plane, and that's just too damn much change!"

Mom liked to tell about Martha Bowman, whose family farmed up on English Prairie, just north of Spring Grove, when my mother was a young girl working at her father's store. Martha learned to drive the family Model-A Ford when she was about sixty years old. She'd load up her hen's eggs in a box and leave her driveway heading south toward town, just creeping along with the Ford in the lowest gear. Mom said Mrs. Bowman would have one wheel on the shoulder and the other about in the middle of her half of the road. If she saw dust boiling up in the distance, indicating the approach of another car, she would pull off the road completely and come to a stop. After the oncoming car had passed and driven a good distance down the road, Martha would ease back onto the gravel and continue heading south to Grandpa's store. As she approached it she would cross the road diagonally and park right next to the store, which was on the northeast corner of the intersection, her Model-A still heading south.

Martha would unload her eggs from the car and take them into the store. Mom and Grandpa would take the eggs to the back and candle them—they had to be clear, without blood spots, or chicks growing inside—to determine how much in groceries could be bartered for the eggs. Then Grandpa would pack the groceries in a box and carry them out to the Ford. After he'd loaded her car, Martha would always ask him, "Now Mr. Weber, would you please turn my car around for me?" Grandpa would turn the car around to the north and Martha would head back to English Prairie, one wheel on the shoulder and one wheel about in the middle of her half of the road. Mom would laugh after she'd finished the story. "I suppose people get around faster than they used to, but I don't know that they're any happier."

Mom didn't like my answering machine much. She was still living in her own house when I left my teaching job and went on the road as a freelance storyteller. The day I purchased the answering machine I had also set up a post office box in town for my business. Since I already had a rural mailbox out in front of my house I figured that each day offered three chances to get good news.

The very next morning I returned from town to find the red light flashing on the answering machine, indicating that calls had come in. These were surely job offers, I thought, invitations to come and tell stories for pay. I had resigned from my tenured teaching position and details like paying the rent and eating regularly were already starting to prey on my mind. I turned the machine dial to REWIND. The tape spun back just a short distance and stopped. "Well," I thought, "probably just one job. But it's a start."

I turned the small dial to PLAYBACK and heard my mother's voice. "This is your mother!" *Click!* She had evidently slammed down the receiver. Now, Mom was always straightforward and to the point and I didn't expect that she would make pleasant small talk to a machine, so I was not particularly surprised by her abruptness. I was pretty busy that day, so I made a mental note to call her in the evening. Well, I forgot.

The following afternoon I came home and the light was flashing again. Of course, I was still hoping for a job, or perhaps several. I turned the dial to REWIND and then PLAYBACK to hear Mom's voice say, "This is your mother, Agnes May!" *Click!* There was such urgency in her voice that I made the decision to go over and see her in person the very next day.

I never got the chance. Early the next morning, she called while I was out jogging. I was tired, sweaty, and feeling pretty darn good as I spun the knob to PLAYBACK for that important job that I knew had to come along eventually. But it was Mom's voice raised to a level of accusation that placed my position in the family somewhere near the brink of disinheritance. "This is your mother, Agnes May, you SOB!" *Click!*Only she did not use the initials but the ripe and zingy words themselves.

First off, I had to note the irony of being tossed this particular epithet by my own mother. Also, it was one thing not to be getting work on the machine but quite another to be cussed out by my dear mom on the official business line. Perhaps I was oversensitive in my economically vulnerable state, because everyone in our family, myself included, was accustomed to Mom's swearing. My father was a horse-trader, but our mother could always outcuss him. In fact, Dad used to make excuses for her to us as children. He'd tell how Mom, the oldest in her family, was put in charge of the rest of the household when her mother died at a young age, so there was never anyone around to "supervise her language." My brother and sisters and I thought it kind of sweet that he made excuses for her.

Looking back, I believe there may have been another reason for her swearing. My mother was the oldest daughter of a prominent businessman. Grandpa Weber owned and operated the general store in town. When Mom worked at the store she would frequently accompany Grandpa to Chicago, where they would order goods. The two of them visited Marshall Field's and other elegant stores and sometimes walked down Adams Street to have lunch at Berghoff's, Chicago's best German restaurant. My grandfather had built his family a new house on Main Street in Spring Grove and owned several lots on Grass Lake for investment purposes. He was a well-respected entrepreneur and was thought of as someone who "had money."

My father, on the other hand, was the second son in a large family of tenant farmers. They rented the farmland on which they made their living. When Mom and Dad got married they "went farming" by renting a place and starting from scratch. They would rent seven different farms during twenty-one years of dairy farming, which meant moving to a different farm about every three years—moving forty or fifty cows, a couple of hundred chickens, ducks, turkeys, and assorted pets, all of the farm machinery, several tons of hay and feed, all of the furniture (purchased at Marshall Field's by my grandfather), and eventually five children.

These tenant farms would usually be run down from several years of neglect and poor harvests, but Mom would dig in with scrub buckets of ammonia water, cans of paint, and rolls of wallpaper. In a week or two those old farmhouses would just sparkle, and the neighbors would stop by and proclaim that this just couldn't be the same house that had been run-down and neglected for years. I've often wondered if it wasn't all those moves, all those old farmhouses with the soiled walls, and the general disruption caused by moving that produced in my mother the ability to swear and curse with the best of them.

In any case, her most recent tirade, recorded on my answering machine, prompted me to call her right away. She answered the phone.

"Hi Mom," I said.

"Who is this?"

"It's Jim."

"Oh, for God's sake!" she laughed. "Well, how are you? I haven't heard from you in a while."

"I've been pretty well. Kind of busy trying to get this new storytelling business going and all," I boasted a little.

"You're telling stories for a living? My God, who would've ever thought it!"

"Well, Mom, I'm going to try, anyway."

"You're not teaching anymore, then?"

"No, Mom, I think I already told you that I wasn't teaching anymore."

"Oh hell! That's right. I just can't seem to remember like I used to. Well, as long as you're doing something you like. There's nothing wrong with being poor just as long as you're clean. We were poor, but you kids were always clean. And we always had enough to eat because we lived on the farm, could grow our own food, even during the Depression. We might have starved to death if we hadn't been on the farm."

"Mom, I don't think I want to hear about that right now." I was thinking about the tenured job and steady paycheck I had given up.

"Are you getting enough to eat?"

"Mom!"

"What?"

"Why have you been calling my answering machine and cursing at me?"

There was quite a long pause at the other end of the line. Then she said, "What answering machine?"

I was puzzled for a moment, but then I realized Mom didn't know that I had an answering machine. It began to take shape in my mind—how it must have happened: my mother would decide to call me. She'd pick up the phone and dial my number. My machine would answer and my message would begin. She'd hear the voice of the son that she'd borne in her own womb, the child that she had brought into the world, say, "Hi! This is Jim." At this point she would start having a conversation with the tape while it was still playing the message.

"This is your mother."

(The tape continued.) "I can't come to the phone right now, so please leave your name—"

"This is Agnes May!" (Spoken with indignation.)

(The tape continued.) "—and I'll be happy to call you back at my earliest convenience." *Beeeeeep!*

"Why, you sonavabitch!" was her salute to the electronic convenience as she banged down the receiver.

Now that I realized her perspective, the cussing seemed pretty understandable. I sought to set things straight. I said, "Mom, it wasn't me. It's a machine that answers the phone when I'm not home. The phone rings. The machine answers with my voice on a tape. When the tape stops, you'll hear a beep and then it will be your turn to talk. You can leave a message for me there on the tape. When you are done speaking, the machine will know that, turn off the recording tape, reset itself, and be ready for the next call. When I get home I will rewind the tape that has recorded my calls, play back all of my messages, hear your message, and call you back. Isn't that a great machine!"

There was another long pause before my mother said, "Am I talking to the machine now?"

As my mother aged, technology continued to march on. The Greek philosophers predicted that technology would be the death of memory, and perhaps the encroachment of modern machines helped wear my mother down. When she was eighty she began to forget, on a fairly regular basis, to turn off her gas cooking stove. She'd search the house all day, sometimes two days, cleaning, looking for the source of what she thought smelled like a dead mouse. Then a neighbor or one of her children would come over, recognize the odor, and rush to turn the stove off and open all the windows.

Then one day she left church in the middle of the mass. Father Anthony watched her walk out of church, a bit unsteady but purposeful as ever, leaning slightly forward, determined to get "where she was goin'." He walked over to her house after church. "Hello, Agnes," he said as she opened the door, looking surprised to see him. "I just wanted to be sure you made it home all right."

"Well, thank you, Father. But I've been here all morning."

Father Anthony smiled and accepted her offer of a cup of coffee. They sat at the kitchen table for a while and chatted. Then Father went home, convinced that he had done what he could.

One day it took her an hour to walk the two blocks from the post office because she kept taking the same wrong street. (There are only two streets in Spring Grove.)

A year or so passed after that visit from our parish priest, and the time came for her to sell her home, the only one she had ever owned. Our family sat in the lawyer's office. She had been in such an office just once before, when she and Dad bought the house. Pen in hand, she looked briefly at the contracts, dropped the pen on the table, and began to cry.

"I feel like I'm signing my life away!" she said. "Why can't I live there anymore? I can't remember what the reasons could be."

"The doctor says you can't live alone," we, her dutiful children, responded. "And you've been forgetting to turn the gas off on the stove, and Father Anthony says that sometimes

you leave church in the middle of mass and he's afraid you might not find your way home, and there was that time you took so long to walk home from the post office, and you've been forgetting to take your blood pressure medicine ...."
We hoped these were reasons enough. We hoped we were doing the right thing. She had almost died that fall, and the doctor felt she needed constant care.

She looked at each one of us thoughtfully and said, "I suppose I *could* blow up the house, but I'm not going to get lost in Spring Grove!" We laughed. She laughed too.

My mother seems more at peace now in the nursing home than she had in all of the years since my father died and her children grew up.

Not long after she moved to Hillcrest, she got a room-mate named Evelyn. The two get along real well, like an old couple who've been farming together for years. At first there were some arguments about whose glasses or shoes or sweater belonged to whom. But after a while they just wore each other's stuff. Evelyn is younger than Mom but very confused, and she doesn't have as many visitors. Mom has more people coming to see her than most of the residents, since the home is close to her children and to where she grew up. She takes day trips with us but never wants to stay overnight away from Hillcrest. About halfway through the trip she begins asking who is going to take her back and when. She resumes the questioning every few minutes, over and over until even the most loyal and understanding relative or friend feels a bit unappreciated. Mom doesn't mean to hurt anyone's feelings, she just can't remember whether she's asked the question or not. Evelyn, her roommate, misses her terribly when she's gone.

Last Valentine's Day I took them cards, one for Evelyn and one for my mother. We sat on the bed and each of them read her card with relish. Mom read hers out loud while Evelyn read quietly. Each put her respective card down as our more mundane conversation replaced the carefully composed violet and lilac sentiments of Hallmark.

"How was supper tonight?" I asked.

"Oh, good!" Mom said. "The food here is always good."

"Yeah," Evelyn said. "It was fine."

"What'd ya have?" I was hoping that we could get on a little bit of a conversational roll. There was silence.

Mom and Evelyn looked at each other. "What did we have? It was good." Mom seemed sure. "I don't know just what it was."

Evelyn turned her head from Mom and looked at the crocheted bedspread that my mother had made years earlier when she turned out these grandmotherly treasures like clockwork, for sons and daughters and nieces and nephews who were getting married or were having their first child. Evelyn smoothed down the wool spread with her hand, not so much trying to recall as feeling embarrassed. Mom looked out the window. Finally they turned back to each other, exchanged glances, and began to laugh. Mom made a motion with her hand, dismissing their inability to answer my question. "We don't remember or know what it is, we just eat it." They giggled shamelessly and with genuine glee.

About then Mom noticed her valentine lying on the bed. She'd forgotten that she had put it there and thought that it was another one. Surprised and pleased, she picked it up and began reading it again, her face beaming with simple joy and appreciation, once more, for the sentimental, flowery words, as if they were the exact truth of her own experience and had been composed just for her. She put the card back on the bed a second time and then noticed Evelyn's card lying next to it. Thinking that someone had brought her yet another valentine she gave a little joyful squeal and set about reading it, too, leaving her own card on the bed near Evelyn, who in turn snatched it up gratefully and began reading.

Evelyn said she hadn't noticed who else had been there but it was nice of them to leave this for her and that she figured she was having a pretty lucky day, all in all. Evelyn read this card happily but to herself because she knew that Agnes had family present.

When it was time for me to go, I kissed my mother and patted Evelyn's hand. When I got to the door and looked back, my mother was sitting alone in her bed, looking distracted. She seemed so small, though she looked neat and kind of pretty as she had just received her weekly, tightly curled hairdo. Her generation had deserted her, I thought, had made her suffer for her vigor and longevity.

I walked back to the side of her bed. "Is everything all right, Mom? Do you need anything?"

"No!" she said, as if it were an outrageous question.

"I like it here. Everyone is so nice. The food is good and I don't have to work, don't have to keep up a house. I worked hard for eighty years. That's enough! Now all I have to do is make the bed."

John Henry

"It's in the Cole Cemetery, at the bottom of the hill along the old fence line." I hadn't known the whereabouts of John Henry's grave until that day.

Tommy and Lorette had been watching "Jeopardy" when I stopped by their small frame house in Wilmot, just over the Wisconsin state line. They seemed pleased with the interruption. Tommy sat in the middle of a stuffed couch, leaning back and a little bit to the side, the cushions on the sofa not giving much support. His face—Irish, ruddy, and round—surrounded blue eyes that surely had twinkled at more than a few jokefests in their day. Tommy's crisp, navy bib overalls were the only new thing in the room. Lorette sat at a secretary along the wall, out of the limelight, listening to Tommy and correcting him with a regularity that was nevertheless completely devoid of malice or even impatience. She wore a calico housedress and glasses that hung around her neck. Her hair was braided in gray pigtails.

Tommy told me again that John Henry was a black man who came to Spring Grove sometime around the turn of the century. Whether he had been emancipated as a young boy or escaped from slavery was unclear. No one knew his age. He said he had been owned by a Mr. Smith and a Mr. Higler, but that Smith had been a cruel master, so when he left the South he took the name of John Henry Higler.

John told Tom that he had first come to Chicago to live, but that things were too "sportin'" there so he found his way along the Milwaukee Road railroad tracks to Spring Grove— where things were a lot less sportin'. He lived most of his life on the Stevens farm. The Stevens family had always lived on the bottom land near Grass Lake. The farm had been homesteaded in the 1840s, some years after the Black Hawk War, and had stayed in the family. They had always had a home so they took in John Henry, who did not.

He was a great help to Mrs. Stevens, who used to joke that she'd rather part with her husband than lose John Henry. John liked working in the house. The Stevens family had a supper table full of children, and John loved them all. He would always take the seat next to the youngest and spoon-feed the baby. On Sundays he'd have the children in has lap while he read them the funny papers. John couldn't read so he made up stories that went with the pictures. Chet Junior always asked John to help him get his boots off at bedtime and for John to tell him a story. Chet would refuse to go to sleep unless he had his bedside visit with John Henry.

It couldn't have been easy for John, being the only black man in the township, although he did have some comforts and people watched out for him. He bought himself a Model-A Ford and he was always welcome down at Jo Brown's corner saloon and pool hall on Saturday nights. Tommy said that sometimes John would stay too late and would ask one of the younger men to drive his car home for him. They'd usually ask, "You all right, John?"

He would say, "Sure, boys, I'm not drunk. I'm just a little nervous."

I left Tommy and Lorette's house and drove south past

the ski hills and crossed the highway while the January sun turned amber and gilded the farms and small, white houses on each side of the road. The sky in front of me was dark blue and chalky. The Cole Cemetery was just three miles from Tommy's. I pulled off the road and parked on a small gravel path that headed straight into a closed iron gate.

It was a hillside graveyard sloping away from the road. There were maybe a hundred or so graves. I made my way down the hill and walked along the edge where the short, frozen grass yielded to taller weeds that were bobbing slightly in the cold wind and glowing orange in the low January sun. There was no fence left but I could see where it had been from the thick brush—osage orange and hawthorn—that grew in a narrow strip that had been spared the lawnmower and the farmer's plow.

I didn't find his grave. At the end of the row of markers I turned back and retraced my steps, stopping at each tombstone to read the inscriptions more carefully. There was no John Henry. As I searched, I thought about this name, which came from the folk legends of the slaves: John Henry, the "steel-drivin' man" who died as a result of that famous battle with the steam drill. I wondered at the battles that our John Henry must have fought. He was the only black man that most of these farmers had ever known. I thought about the loneliness. I remember one of the Stevenses telling me that John would stay in the kitchen in his rocking chair after the children were put to bed. They'd ask him to come sit in the living room with them, but he'd always decline.

Tommy told me that once during threshing time, two day laborers took an oil can and squirted John Henry, who was standing below them next to the grain stack. He got pretty filthy, all covered with the sticky oil and the chaff from the grain. Tommy said, "He was a mess, all itchy and slick from that oil, but he didn't say much. John never liked to make trouble, never wanted to bother anybody. When

Mr. Stevens found out about it at the noon meal he fired those two fellas on the spot." With this last remark Tommy poked at the air with a small, liver-spotted fist, his thumbnail a gun-metal blue marker, to emphasize his point. He seemed vindicated by Mr. Stevens's administration of sure and fast justice.

I remembered an old black man named Abraham who used to come to our farm to buy scrap iron. One day, while I was home alone I sold my pile of iron to him for a dollar. He was a friendly guy and had done business with me just like I was the man of the house, even though I was only seven. He offered me a dollar and a half for the scrap and I agreed. He gave me a dollar and was reaching into his pocket for the rest of the money but I told him to keep the change, as I had often heard my father say.

I got in some trouble for this when my older sisters got home. They said I had done a foolish thing. I cried and hid under the bed for a good long time until I figured everyone in the family would be so worried about me that I wouldn't be in too much trouble when I finally came out. The scrap pile was about the only thing I owned and I had been looking forward to selling it for months. But I could tell that there was something else about this ill-fated business transaction that was embarrassing. Though nothing was spoken, I sensed that I should be more ashamed because I had been bested in the trade by a black man.

Years after John Henry's death, I recalled my mother saying that some of our relatives didn't approve of John dancing with my aunts and cousins at the barn dances. I wondered what other demons I might come across as I tracked down these events of my life and community. At that moment, the narrative planks that I was laying across this bridge to my past seemed to flow over muddy, angry waters.

Finally, I gave up my search for John's tombstone. I figured that he was given a pauper's burial, maybe a wooden cross, and that nothing remained of it. I was starting back up the hill when I saw it, almost stumbled over it there at my feet. It was a small but very proper granite headstone, and it read JOHN HENRY HIGLER. There was no birthdate, since accurate birth records for slaves were rare, but it stated that he had died in 1946, the same year that my grandfather had died and a year before I was born. In front of the grave, lighting up a little bit of the winter grayness around it, was a bright red plastic geranium.

John didn't have any family in the area as far as anyone knew, so I asked around to see who might have placed that flower on the forty-year-old grave. Though I never found out for sure, the trail pointed to a couple of the old farm families. I finally reasoned that it didn't matter who had done it. What did seem important was that John and those farmers had forged friendships that ignored the differences of race, culture, and geography, and that testimony to those bonds stood there before me in the Cole Cemetery. The store-bought flower with the plastic petals hinted at a warm spring day and dotted the winter snow with a blood-red bloom.

Mourning Dove

*F*ifty-six frogs died in Spring Grove the summer of 1957. My friends and I counted them. Each day there was a bit less croaking and fewer *ker-plunk*s as frogs jumped into the water, warned by the slight shaking of the ground under their delicate feet as we stepped along the streambank. The frogs lived in a stream that widened and slowed a bit to form a little stagnant pool covered with algae and duckweed. The frog hole was behind St. Peter's Church, just upstream from where the little creek joined with a slightly larger branch about a hundred feet to the west, ran through a culvert under Main Street, and emptied into the lazy-traveling, muddy Nippersink.

The frog place grew quieter with the passage of summer days, and the dead frogs accumulated among the weeds and clouded the water. Some of the decaying frogs lay on their backs, their white bellies tangled in the green algae. Other carcasses seemed to stand in the water, their legs spread-eagled, their toes fanned like amphibian minstrel singers, their pink entrails snaking in the current, sometimes wrapping around their bobbing torsos like filmy scarves.

After it stood quiet for a few days, my friends and I stopped going to the pond. We looked for other things to shoot with our BB guns. Recalling this slaughter now, as I look back over the years, I am ashamed and unable to understand the cruelty and calm, workmanlike manner in which my friends and I carried out the slaughter of this big-eyed, innocent bunch of God's offspring, who no doubt had entertained their own designs for that summmer, their own piece of destiny to live out.

We loved our BB guns. The smooth wooden stock of my Daisy as it pressed against my cheek was a strange joy, a uniting of machine and human that rivaled the devotion that I felt for my bicycle. I loved loading it with the small, perfectly round, bright copper shot, hearing each one of them chime and peel as it dropped down the long, steel cylinder that ran underneath the barrel of the gun.

That the frogs should suffer so horribly for my dedication to this toylike killing machine preyed only a little upon my conscience. I remember confessing my serial amphibicide to our priest, who seemed hardly concerned. Assuring me that it was only a venial and therefore not a serious sin, he did remind me that I should always "eat whatever I kill." This was a rural maxim that I was more than willing to live by, since my chief desire at the time was to live like primitive man. Raw meat, still pulsing as I devoured it, would have been, at least in my imagination, the preferred nourishment, although I was hesitant to give up my mother's cinnamon rolls and German coffeecake. And next to becoming a priest or bishop, I thought pursuing wild game to feed myself and my tribe would be the best possible job. So after my discussion with the priest, my friends and I tried to roast the frog legs over a fire, but we never quite mastered their preparation.

My brother, Paul, had given me the gun for Christmas when I was nine. It was a great surprise since it was not the kind of present I was used to getting from my parents. Paul was single and making a lot of money working construction at the time. He was twenty-two years old, a great teller of jokes, and the most fun of anyone in my family. Sometimes he'd talk in made-up language or just say things that made no sense at all. "Hey, Paul, where did you work today?" I'd ask. "Cuba," he'd say for no reason.

I knew he didn't work in Cuba, but compared to the lives of the local farmers and clerks in town, his construction job was adventurous, taking him all over two or three counties. It might as well have been Cuba, or Cancun, or Madagascar to me, and I guess that's why he said it.

Christmas Day we both wanted to try out the gun, so before dinner we took it outside. Paul carried the gun, loaded with sixty BBs. We had only walked a short way when he snapped the gun to his shoulder and fired. A loud, spring-loaded *puff* with a *ping* at the end resounded from the barrel of the gun, along with a small spray of oil. I followed the line of the gun barrel with my eyes and saw a chunk of feathers and pink flesh leap from a small spot just above the tiny, thin leg of a sparrow that was hunkering down on our grape arbor, trying to keep warm. Despite what was surely a mortal wound, the little bird flew away.

"Pretty powerful," my brother said.

A real gun, I thought.

We went back into the house for Christmas Day dinner. All during the meal I thought about my Daisy gun. At the time I didn't see any conflict with the name Daisy and its deadly function. My father eyed the gun lying under the Christmas tree. I told him about the sparrow. He said, "Don't be killing any wrens or robins or barn swallows, now." Dad was suspicious, and perhaps sought some limit to the destruction he foresaw.

After dinner I walked out of the house, my gun grasped in both hands—my right hand on the grip near the trigger, my left hand cradling the barrel. This efficient carrying position would allow me to snap the gun to my shoulder and fire in a split second. I knew this position from watching all of the hunting shows on the television and from reading my *Field and Stream* magazines. I wasn't sure what it was that I needed to be so ready to shoot, but the critical thing was to be prepared.

Once I gained possession of that unexpected gun, my world seemed truly wild. There was a suspense and purpose to my walks in the woods, a sense of anticipation that I had only before experienced in my daydreams about hunting and wilderness survival. I felt like one of the young men in *Boy Hunters,* my favorite adventure series. For I was old enough, man enough, to go into the world to hunt. Having a gun, any gun, in the wild meant that I was a hunter. And being a hunter somehow connected me with the earliest of men whose very lives depended upon their ability to forge a relationship with nature. All of my life I had envied the men who had had the good fortune to live in frontier times.

I was now an equal to the animals. I now lived in a world with them, close to them. Everything seemed a part of this transformation, from the smell of the frozen ground to the feel of the north wind on my cheek, a wind that I knew had blown from an even wilder place. I was sure that I could live off the land if I had to, that I could be self-sufficient.

I shudder now to think of the small creatures that fell victim to this ethic of country mythology that sought such a union with nature. The boys that I knew who loved the woods were also hunters. Maybe if we could have actually experienced the wild and elemental—crawled inside the skin of an animal for a few days or weeks—we wouldn't have felt the need to hunt.

Talking among ourselves, we might have said, "I'm really looking forward to this week because I get to be a hawk; I get to soar, to glide over the prairies, head swinging from side to side seeing everything that I wish to see, fearing nothing." Or, "I get to be a fox and see what it's like to hunt for my supper and trot along fence lines and down trails through the underbrush, smelling the musky scents of a hundred different creatures that have passed this way in the smoky, crystalline moonlight." Or, "Tomorrow I'm going to be a catfish and explore the creek and see for myself what goes on beneath those swirling brown waters, see it for myself with my own sleepy yellow eyes." If we could have been shape-shifters, we wouldn't have wanted guns.

Instead, our lives felt regimented and closely guarded by community elders, by the priest and nuns, and, most of all, by our own consciences, which had been carefully chiseled by the dogmas of the church. So to be out in the woods was to escape from "town," to be where the laws of nature ruled, where the sights, sounds, and smells were so overpowering that notions of rigid order and threats of eternal perdition seemed, at least temporarily, remote and of no importance. Then too, the violence that little boys come to know, from playground drummings by older boys to the sometimes brutal spankings at school, was passed on in one form or another to the wild, living things we encountered as hunters.

I don't think the men had anywhere to escape either. Men that I grew up around did not go walking in the woods. This was looked upon as a weakness, as a peculiarity that might set one apart from friends, might make one seem out of place and even be cause for banishment.

But a hunter arising at the crack of dawn on a cold late October morning was a whole different matter. A hunter tumbling out of his warm bed in time to sit in a cold blind and watch the eastern sky turn rosy and listen to the honking of geese gathering for their southern trek was understood, even admired. And such actions made one's company desirable. Never mind the real reason that they went, that the sight of the coral streak in the eastern sky and the sounds of night becoming day so struck these tough men that they were rendered speechless among their buddies. They treasured these moments, set apart, away from the responsibilities of job and family, to immerse themselves in the immediacy of great natural forces, to hold silent vigil in the cattails as the sun appeared to emerge out of the black pond water. And of course, because they were hunters, no one could blame them for these soft and suspicous sensibilities.

In those days with my first gun, there was only a fluttering in my chest and a yearning to take to the field. That Christmas afternoon I walked alone through the snow, my eyes like a hawk's, inspecting every rabbit track, watching for the slightest movement in the grass, oblivious to the fact that a Daisy air rifle was not really made for hunting but rather for target practice. No matter, it was a gun!

It was a swath of minor destruction that I cut that winter, spring, and summer with my new BB gun. I still dream, at times, that I face a gentle, pantheistic god on my own judgment day. The two of us gaze upon an illusory and gossamer six-foot pile of dead sparrows, blackbirds, frogs, mice, and gophers—their arms, whiskers, and legs jutting in every direction—all felled by the tiny copper cannonballs that belched from my sweet Daisy. And the great spirit asks one inevitable question: "Why did you do it? You must have had a reason to kill so many times." And after an entire lifetime of reflection I am only able to say, "I don't know."

But an event occurred late that first summer of my BB gun that caused me to stop and take pause, caused me to wonder, and to question this ardent devotion to the hunt. It was mid-August, humid and hot. A storm was amassing somewhere in the thick slate sky, sending low grumblings across the prairie. There was a wet heaviness to the air that gave it substance and content, as if on these last great days of summer a truth—urgent and close, perhaps a warning—was about to be revealed. The rumbling of the storm and the dropping of the atmospheric pressure caused something in the marrow of my bones to change, to become alert, perhaps to rise toward the surface of my skin in a kind of osmosis, flowing toward the outside, toward the storm that was coming.

That day a mourning dove sat on the telephone wire in front of our house. There is something about the close hours before a summer storm that moves these delicate creatures to *cooooo* all of the sorrow of the world, to puff their sweet breasts and emit an arresting and heartbreaking sound that becomes the lovely cello of the orchestra that is summer in the country. But to me, the call of the dove also hinted at a mystery of nature and of its wild places that humans are teased with but can never inhabit.

I had never shot a dove. That day, however, something about its boldness, there on the wire, and the opportunity to possess such a beautiful bird, and the fear that I would lose this oportunity, made me draw the gun slowly up to my cheek and aim it carefully, my arm steady, cradling the underside of the gun barrel. I held my breath and squeezed the trigger. I heard the thump of the pellet as it struck the bird's wing. The dove tumbled to the ground, wings and legs flailing. No longer graceful, the bird tossed and flipped itself along the ground trying to escape its tormentor—the thing that was burning in its wing. Dust and small stones collected in its sleek feathers. The graceful bird that only a moment ago had been eloquently serenading a hot, musky morning was now convulsing in the dirt. It could not fly from this predicament, could not dart through the trees at breakneck speed as it was accustomed to doing.

My heart sank. I knew immediately that I had done something horrible. I caught the bird and held it in my hands. I gently pressed the broken wing to its body. The wing made a grating sound as the bird squirmed in my hand, its heart pulsing in my own small palm. *What's such a bird to do without a wing?* I thought.

My mind was reeling. I wished this bird back up into the sky. I prayed for this bird to return to its world, untainted by its encounter with me, with human contact. It was no longer mysterious and wild. In the space of one second I had tamed it. I had brought it into my world, brought to it this humiliation.

I carried it to the little barn behind our house. Inside I looked for a crate or a box, something to nurse the bird in, though I didn't know how. I found a basket with a cover and put the dove in it. I pressed some leaves against the wing that was now bleeding steadily, a bright blood filled with life and flight draining away. I knew that this blood, now dripping onto the concrete floor, contained the mystery that caused the bird to sing in the haunting tones that I loved.

As the dove began its death rattle, the damaged wing flapped in a succession of short, quick beats, as though it was waving goodbye to me. I almost felt forgiven for a moment but that feeling ebbed to heartsickness for what now seemed a personal loss. Finally, the bird lay still. Its life passed while I stood vigil over the waste that I had caused, my regret and sorrow not only meaningless but confirming my own guilt and inability to reverse my fortunes. The hunter is empty and powerless after the kill. There is the thrilling hope of capturing the wildness only when the animal is alive. After its death there is only a vacuum because there is no way to bring the life back, to continue the chase. I could never make that dove fly again. Death is a one-way trip. And the predator is left empty. So real hunters always eat their prey to fill the void.

My killing spree ended that day. I put my BB gun in the back of my closet. The mourning dove had cooed that hot and hazy August day, foretelling the thunderstorm but never understanding the storm that brewed inside a small boy.

Horse Snot

I learned to serve mass the first year that my family moved into Spring Grove. We sold the farming business and moved into a house only two doors from the church, so while some boys had to trudge through the snow early on winter mornings or have their parents drive them, I would just run across the back yard to the side door of the church into the boys' sacristy, where I dressed for the service. My traveling time was about sixty seconds or less. I was often called when other boys missed their scheduled times. The convent where our teaching nuns lived was right next door, between our house and the church. If the scheduled altar boy for the morning daily mass did not show up, Sister Leon, who was in charge of the altar boys, would open her window and holler for me. I'd hear my name, jump out of bed, and run downstairs, dressing on the way. I'd splash some cold water on my face, no time to brush my teeth—which was risky anyway. It might break the Eucharistic Fast. Fasting was prescribed by the church from midnight to the time of communion, and some of us took this so literally that even a taste of

Pepsodent was to be feared. Then I'd run out the door—a veritable Holy Roman Minuteman.

After some success at serving mass, I began to set certain goals for myself. The first, of course, was to learn Latin. Latin was the official language of the Catholic liturgy—the mass and practically all of the sacred devotions were said in Latin. We altar boys learned our Latin from books with phonetic English pronunciations. We were well-drilled by Sister Leon, and we sounded great, but we had very little idea what we were saying. We were told that in spite of the fact that Latin was a "dead language," it was used in every Catholic church in the world, so that we could go into a Catholic Church anywhere and recognize the service, a universality hailed by our religious instructors as a great advantage. This meant we Spring Grovers, most of whom had never been out of McHenry County (and then only to take the bus to the Chicago Cubs or White Sox baseball game), could go to any Catholic church in the world and not understand what was being said by the priest, just like we didn't understand our priest's Latin prayers right here at home. The church of my youth was famous for these curious comforts.

By the time I was ten years old, I could recite my memorized Latin perfectly. I had remained faithful to my serving schedule and was gaining a reputation as a "utility player"—filling in at a moment's notice when less diligent servers missed their turns.

It was fitting, then, that I should entertain higher aspirations. I began planning for the future, reasoning that if I continued this high level of performance and if I endeavored to be a "good boy," I had a chance, by the time I would enter eighth grade, to become Most Valuable Altar Boy. At St. Peter's you knew that you had been appointed the Most Valuable Altar Boy—the MVAB—if, during your eighth-grade school year, you were chosen to carry the thurible—or, as it was commonly called, censer—during Midnight

High Mass on Christmas Eve.

The censer was an ornate, golden urn. It hung from several chains that were fastened to its top and sides in such a way as to keep it in an upright position while it was swung back and forth by the head altar boy or priest. It needed to be kept moving because it held a small cup that in turn held a piece of burning charcoal. This constant motion allowed air to move through small vents in the side of the censer and over the charcoal, keeping it fired and ready for its eventual devotional use.

At a certain time during the mass, the priest would turn to the altar boys and call a huddle. All of the altar boys would gather around. The MVAB would pull the middle chain on the censer, causing the lid to lift, exposing the red-hot coal. The priest would turn to the runner-up for MVAB, who carried the frankincense in a small box that we called a boat. Father would use a golden spoon to scoop out a portion of incense, sprinkle it on the hot coal and, as my dad used to say, "The whole contraption would smoke like hell!"

The MVAB would let loose of the middle chain, allowing the lid to clank back into position, and hand the thurible back to the priest as thick smoke billowed out of all sides. The priest would then incense the altar, walking its length, swinging the censer. He'd hand it back to the MVAB, who would wave the thurible at the priest in the prescribed ritualistic manner and then take it to the communion rail. Facing the assembled worshipers, with the thurible now belching smoke like a steam locomotive on an uphill grade, he would "incense the congregation."

The most fun of the entire ritual was incensing the priest. We servers had a bit of lore that was passed orally and in secret from one MVAB to the next, the substance of which was that a certain twist of the wrist and dip of the elbow could direct a compact but substantial cloud of "holy smoke" right up the priest's nostrils. Being MVAB was the best job in the parish.

Another advantage to being most valuable was a clearance to carry matches. A boy with a pack of matches and a pocketknife could literally swagger through life. Back in those more innocent days on the playground, before drugs and pornography, a boy might say to a friend, "Hey, you wanna see some matches?"

"Wow! Where'd ya get 'em?"

"They're mine," would be the confident reply of the MVAB. "I use them in church. Let's go burn a dead ant!"

Of course, there was no hope of being chosen most valuable unless one was considered by the nuns to be a good boy. Given the many advantages of "MVABdom," my altar boy friends and I were trying our best to be good.

But there were more important reasons to be good as well. The sisters and priests had warned us about the fires of hell on the one hand, and the rewards of heaven on the other. I choose here not to recount the descriptions of hell for fear that the gruesome details would distress and distract the reader from the rest of the story, which this writer modestly hopes will be somewhat more humorous than the specter of hot bubbling flesh in the eternal furnaces.

I must, however, return to the 1950s, pre-Vatican II, Catholic understanding of heaven. We were often told that heaven was like a great banquet hall or theater, but with no general seating—and certainly no free admission. The quality of one's seat depended upon the relative virtue of the life one had led.

The nuns and priests explained that in the far corner, or the back row, or perhaps at the end of the table, were the people who had just barely made it into heaven by the skin of their teeth. They had led holy but boring lives.

In the middle section of heaven were the martyrs. Being a martyr was no small thing. The martyrs were the Christians who had been executed because of their faith, men and women who chose to die rather than deny their beliefs. Most of the apostles were martyrs. Christians who were thrown to the lions were martyrs. Being a martyr meant that you had a pretty good place in heaven, more jewels in your heavenly crown, so to speak.

But the very best places in heaven, right up in front, or seated at the table, close to God, were reserved for the virgin martyrs, those people who had been killed for professing their faith before they had sex. It didn't give you much to look forward to, but we were taught that life on this earth didn't matter anyhow.

I was ten years old, a certified virgin. I was halfway there!

I was trying so hard to become St. Peter's Most Valuable Altar Boy that I devoted practically every waking moment to the pursuit of this ideal: I said my daily prayers; attended mass every morning, sometimes twice on Sundays; confessed my sins to the priest every Saturday night; and made lots of visits to the church, just to say hello to God. I even put pebbles in my shoes so that I could, in some small way, suffer as Christ had suffered. Later I found out that Jesus had worn sandals and probably had never had a pebble caught in his shoe—no pebble problem whatsoever. Upon learning this, I stopped using pebbles immediately. I never sought to be Christlike in my choice of footwear, since not even religious fanatics were allowed to wear sandals in Spring Grove without enduring the scorn of society.

It was during my pebble period, I think, that word got around town that I was a "goody-goody." And one day, I was set up.

It was a Saturday, and I was walking to the store when I noticed Duane Weidner and Timmy Bauer leaning up against Vic Blink's fence. I should have known that something was up because Duane had a reputation in town. He was a couple years older than the rest of us and was known for playing tricks and teasing younger boys. Once when I was eight, he convinced me and several of my friends that hot road tar, rolled into a ball and chewed for several minutes, was very good for cleaning the teeth; it seemed like a good idea at the time. He was also known for talking about what the nuns called "impure thoughts," which most of us knew had something to do with sins against the sixth commandment. Sister Leon told one eighth-grader that Duane thought of himself as a missionary from an order of weirdos.

Anyway, just as I was passing the two of them that day, Duane said, "Hey Timmy, what are you going to do tonight?"

Timmy, who was younger than I was at the time, replied by saying the *F*-word, whereupon Duane began laughing hysterically.

Now I had never heard a word such as that and had no idea what it meant, but not wanting to appear ignorant and uncool, I feigned a knowing little chuckle and bolted to the store. I bought the groceries my mother wanted and returned home, still confused.

It was the best time of the week—Saturday afternoon. Mom had been baking all day, and the house was filled with the aroma of freshly baked bread. No chocolate factory, no garden of lilacs, no fragrance on earth so comforts the senses as the smell of baked bread in your own house. After mass on Sundays, all my relatives would stop over. We'd sit around the kitchen table, tell jokes, stories, and eat the cinnamon rolls, German coffeecake, and fresh bread and rolls that my mother had made the day before.

When I walked into the kitchen with my bag of groceries, breads and coffeecakes were cooling on the counter and Mom was kneading a football-sized mound of dough on the kitchen table. She'd pick up the dough with one hand, slap some flour on the table with the other one so the heavy batter wouldn't stick, slam the ball of precious, sticky stuff back down with a thump, and start at it again with both fists.

I cut myself a slice of hot bread, spread some butter on it, and set it down on the counter to watch the butter melt. As I watched the butter form a little yellow puddle of sunshine on the white, steaming bread, my thoughts returned to Duane and Timmy. So I decided to ask my mother what the *F*-word meant, using the word exactly as Timmy had pronounced it.

"Where did you hear that!" she demanded, abruptly halting her bread-kneading in mid-thump.

I told her exactly what had happened, repeating the *F*-word again, slowly, clearly, paying particular attention to those strong closing consonants: *"—ck!"*

"I heard you the first time!" She slapped the bread dough back on the table and began to knead it ferociously.

Both hands! Slapping the flour onto the table, flipping the dough, slapping the flour. "That's a filthy and disgusting way to talk," she said, as she gave the dough another punch and dusted it again with a big handful of flour. Her face was all red and there was a near whiteout condition in the kitchen—flour dust everywhere.

I didn't want to know anymore what the *F*-word meant. I just wanted to get out of there as fast as I could. So I did. I ran out of the kitchen and through the dining room, opened the screen door, and burst out onto the porch. Even though I was safe again, I looked back into the kitchen.

Out of the cloud of flour that enveloped the room, I heard my mother's voice say, "Well, you know, it's like horses breeding."

Now she was clearly doing the best she could. She knew that I loved horses and she was trying to give me a frame of reference. We had kept our horses when we moved to town and, in fact, my horse had just had a foal, so I knew a little bit about where baby horses came from and I was all for it—thought it was a miracle. If I had only heard her right,

things might have been different. Maybe the distance between the porch and the kitchen distorted her words. Maybe
her words were muffled because my own ears were ringing
with embarrassment, or perhaps the sound waves from my
mother's voice were ricocheting off of the flour molecules in
the air, because I could have sworn my mother said, "It's like
horses breathing."

This made no sense, of course, but I was anxious to get
out of the situation, so I said, "Right!" and ran down the
porch steps and out to the street. I walked around town all
day thinking to myself, "Horses breathe, all animals breathe,
people breathe, everybody breathes! What could be 'filthy
and disgusting' about a horse breathing?" Then I remembered something about horses.

My father loved to trade horses. Every once in a while
he would "get the worst of it" in a horse trade and get stuck
with a horse that had the heaves—a respiratory disease that
caused the horse to breath irregularly. If such a horse was fed
dusty hay or grain, it would go into a coughing spasm. The
horse's sides would heave. It would sneeze and snort, and
green, mucous-like stuff would come out of its nose—that's
when I figured out what the *F*-word meant! The *F*-word
must mean HORSE SNOT! Now *that's* pretty filthy and
disgusting!

Armed with this knowledge, I sallied forth into puberty
with what I considered to be my worldly confidence intact,
holding on to this misconception for longer than I care to
admit. But after a few years I began to experience what the
psychologists call cognitive dissonance. For I would place
the idea, horse snot, in the context of whatever situation I
heard the *F*-word used in. And I had to admit this strategy
wasn't working out very well.

For instance, during a Little League game, one of my
friends would strike out, throw the bat down, and say,
"Horse snot!" Or someone might say, "I ran my bicycle into

a tree and horse-snotted-up the fender." The worst was when a high-school senior would come up to me, a lowly freshman, and say, "Hey squirt! Go horse-snot yourself!" What a disgusting concept for a farm boy!

Unable to stand the confusion, I went to my best friend and neighbor, Ned Schmidt. He was a Protestant and got to go to all of those B- and C-rated movies that we Catholic boys and girls were forbidden to see by the Catholic Legion of Decency, which published a new list of taboo movies each month. (Oh, that list! Just reading the names was a thrill: *I, A Camera; Jules and Jim; Never On Sunday.* Our imaginations conjured up deliciously sinful images that the silver screen could never have delivered!)

Ned went to all those forbidden movies starring Rock Hudson and Doris Day; thus he possessed solid information about sexuality—gleaned from these very realistic movies—that I lacked. I asked him to tell me the truth about the *F*-word, and he did. The truth was even more filthy and disgusting than anything I had heard up until then.

Of course, I don't feel this way anymore.

Prince

*H*aving grown up on a farm, I now take it upon myself to debunk the many myths and falsehoods that have arisen about farm life during the post-World War II urbanization of America. It is my desire to address specifically the manner in which farm boys are schooled in the arts of animal husbandry and species procreation.

Many untruths have arisen among the uninformed and urbane, the most odious of which is the mistaken notion that farm boys learn about the birds and the bees, the facts of life—alas sexuality—in a relaxed, natural way, by watching God's creatures daily display their physical affection for one another, all amongst the innocence and grandeur of country environs, isolated from and untainted by the widespread sin and debauchery so valiantly endured by their city cousins.

This whole notion that farm children are sophisticated in these matters of the flesh is, most assuredly, a lot of bull! (Incidently, if you've ever seen a lot of bull—a bull, that is, with love on his mind—innocence and grandeur is not what prevails upon the memory. Well, grandeur perhaps, but not innocence.)

The truth of the matter is that when it came to information about the birds and the bees, I for one was a farm boy steeped in agrarian ignorance of the most profound and disordered sort. This was not due to a lack of interest on my part. I endeavored to make use of the resources that were available. But the bees were small and fast, thereby discouraging close examination, while the birds were scarce on the prairie and usually observed at great distances. Consequently, I did, instead, pay a good deal of attention to our barnyard animals, without guidance, however, and with no useful biological information resulting from my systematic surveillance.

For example, I remember watching our barnyard Muscovy ducks. The large, scarlet-faced males would pounce on the smaller, more delicate females and straddle them in such a way as to cause their feathered mates to be squashed into the dust and the dirt. Though I now know that I was witnessing a romantic tryst, it didn't look like a fair fight to me. It was my routine custom, under such circumstances, to wallop the preoccupied, passionate, and eventually startled male duck over the head with a broom or snow shovel, whichever was handy, until he was forced to abandon what I thought to be his unfair position, be it missionary or otherwise.

Did my parents use these demonstrations of barnyard libido to instruct me in the Divine Plan? To explain the mysteries of creation and perhaps attempt to forewarn me about the tyrannical power of hormones? No! My father would only say, in a gruff voice, "Leave 'em alone!" No explanation, just, "Leave 'em alone!"

Likewise, I was required to stay out of the barn when our neighbor brought his stallion over to visit our mare. Now this was very peculiar, since the only other times I'd been banned from the barn were when my father and uncles butchered a steer. I knew what happened on those occasions:

the steer would walk into the barn on four legs and come out in little white packages, and my mother would cook fresh beef liver and tongue for supper.

So when our neighbor's stock truck rolled into the yard and his big stallion came prancing down the loading ramp, my friends and I would observe this magnificent beast with great interest. The stud horse would be snorting, whinnying, and rolling his eyes, nostrils flared and sniffing the air, flanks dripping with sweat. It would take two men, each with a chain lead strap tied to the stallion's halter, just to maneuver him from the truck to the barn.

Since we youngsters had never seen an animal so agitated, we assumed that the stallion had found out what went on in the barn, knew about those steers who'd come out in little white packages! We decided that his temperament was probably appropriate, given his desperate situation, what with it being the last few moments of his life and all.

But a short time later our theories would need recalculating, when the very same stallion emerged from the barn relaxed, calm, and satisfied. There was nothing for us to conclude but that he was happy to be alive and feeling fortunate that he had not been butchered after all.

It would be impossible to figure when or how I would have learned the shocking but nevertheless sublime truth about reproduction had my family stayed on the farm. But, for better or worse, our farming operation succumbed to the dismal agricultural business climate of the fifties, so we moved into Spring Grove—a town of two hundred people, where I learned the facts of life in the customary manner. I gained my instruction "on the streets"; in the case of Spring Grove, the exact location of this pivotal event in my pre-pubescent education would have been either Blivin Street or Main Street, there being only two streets in the municipality.

As my adolescence approached, I digested every bit of information I could gather from Spring Grove's various street philosophers. Having no direct data from personal experience, I was operating in a baffling state of relative ignorance.

When I was thirteen I would often accompany my father to his job caring for the brood mares on a Lipizzan horse farm. Once again I was in a position to observe the courtship rituals of the most noble of my barnyard friends. I took every opportunity to scrutinize the breeding program that this farm employed in order to produce these valuable Austrian steeds.

Now the program revolved around the mares, who were only capable of conception at certain times of the year. These females had no interest whatsoever in a stallion's attentions other than during these fertile times. In fact, more than one enthusiastic stud horse had received a good kick in the head, sometimes literally knocking his nose out of joint in the process, for showing interest at the wrong time of a mare's biological cycle. Stallions are, on the other hand, a "horse of a different color," so to speak—always interested, always ready, ever burdened with their primordial instinct to enrich the gene pool.

Now, given the dangerous nature of these proceedings, the horse breeders who managed these herds were determined to avoid the risk of injury to a valuable stallion by making absolutely certain that a mare was ready. Therefore they employed a second stallion to act as a teaser. The job of the teaser was to approach the mare with the usual enthusiasm. The mare would then respond with an appropriate gesture—sometimes friendly, other times brutally hostile—depending upon her particular biological predisposition at the time.

The teaser on the Temple Lipizzan Farm was a stallion named Prince. He was a magnificent animal: his gray dapples the color of pewter; his small, delicate head, which he carried high and alert on his great, muscled, arched neck, was ghostly white; his eyes large, doe-like, intelligent. Prince's only drawback was that he was not a full-blooded Lipizzan. In fact Prince had no papers to confirm, or even suggest, what bloodline or combination of bloodlines had spawned such beauty.

Temple Smith, the owner of the farm, was a Chicago industrialist who had fallen in love with the Lipizzan breed and the story of how they were saved from the invading Nazi forces during World War II. An ancient lineage, these horses were first bred for battle and are still trained to execute the powerful and elegant leaps that made them impressive cavalry mounts in the midst of battle. In later times they were bred for show and were the toast of the Hapsburg monarchy, which kept them performing at the famous Vienna Riding School, where a select group of Lipizzans still can be seen.

Having decided to build a herd, Temple was in Austria buying Lipizzans when he spotted Prince pulling a farmer's manure wagon. My father told me this story the first time I saw Prince. I remember being fascinated and curious about Europe, and about Austria in particular. I reasoned that it must be a wonderful and elegant country if such a magnificent animal would be pulling a lowly peasant's manure spreader!

Temple was so stunned with the beauty of this dapple gray that he purchased Prince on the spot, rescuing him from a life of toil and obscurity, only to damn him, as it turned out, to one of extreme frustration. For Prince was to become perhaps the most beautiful teaser ever to grace a horse farm.

In the execution of his duties at Temple Farms, Prince anxiously awaited the presentation of a mare for weeks and months at a time. When the moment finally arrived, he would be led prancing out of his stall, excited but nevertheless a perfect gentleman, requiring only one man to control him, anticipating what he surely thought would be a romantic interlude appropriate for a male horse of his mythic beauty and proportion. In this expectation Prince was, perhaps, the most pitiable of eternal optimists.

Rushing up to his waiting flower of a filly, he would, more often than not, be greeted by a loud squeal as the insulted and misunderstood mare wheeled her rear end in his direction and delivered a well-aimed hoof to that beautiful jaw. Prince would leap backward, amazed and terribly humiliated, then hang his head and walk docilely back to his stall, hardly needing anyone to lead him.

Worse were the occasions when the winsome and fickle mare did show an interest. She'd nuzzle Prince affectionately and sniff him with purpose and intent, and just as she began to maneuver him toward her garden of secret delights (the business end of the operation, from her owner's point of view), Prince would begin to entertain the possibility that his long string of bad luck was coming to an end, only to have his handler jerk on the lead strap and pull the would-be suitor away from the mare and back toward his stall. Prince would bolt, rear, and spin around to look at the mare, who would also be whinnying her objections as he was hauled away by two or three men.

Prince's job was done, and his services, though desired by the mare, were not needed. A purebred Lipizzan stallion—we'll call him Big Hans—who, compared to Prince, was jugheaded and awkward in appearance, would be led from the other side of the barn to consummate the proceedings and reap the rewards attendant to the mare's aroused condition. Prince, dejected, would be back in his stall, treated perhaps to an extra ration of oats for his trouble.

So this farm boy had, at last, learned something about love from the creatures of the agrarian community. This lesson was so bitter, however, that it left me jaded and discouraged with country life. I found those barnyard escapades to be of the most fowl nature, with a preponderance of aggression and very little cuddling, and they provided no helpful clues to how to develop a suitable courtship strategy of my own. So to those citified romantics for whom farm life conjures up notions of profound and innocent passion, I say: "Go ask a duck."

It made matters worse that during my early dealings in romance, I would, time and again, have cause to identify with the plight of Prince, the earnest and gentlemanly stallion, who, though full of oats, was nevertheless continually frustrated in matters of love.

Sister Maria

I wanted to be noticed. Most teenagers do, I suppose. But I was from St. Peter's Parish in Spring Grove, which made being noticed even more important. We were the smallest parish in the county, located in the northernmost reaches of Illinois, near the Wisconsin state line, which placed us about one and a half hour's drive from Chicago. After I graduated from our parish elementary school, I went to high school at Marian Central in Woodstock. It was the only Catholic high school in the county, so it not only drew students from Woodstock but from miles around, including the larger towns like McHenry and Crystal Lake. The largest towns were at the southeastern end of the county and closer to Chicago. These parishes were bigger and each of them sent many more students to Marian than did St. Peter's.

Most of the kids from these larger parishes went to high school with all or most of their friends. This was usually not true for those of us from St. Peter's. None of my best chums went to Marian and the few "Grovers" (Spring Grove residents) who were there got thinly scattered among the classes and cliques from the big parishes. We were dealt the social challenge of infiltrating established circles of friends.

My first year of high school I thought that I might have the inside track at getting noticed because I had finished second in the annual Knights of Columbus Christopher Columbus Essay Contest. I figured that this would bring me lots of attention because those Knights of Columbus really knew how to dress. They wore long, black, satin capes lined in red and hats with white ostrich plumes that looked remarkably like the one worn by Mr. Christian in *Mutiny on the Bounty*. But the true badge of their status, the thing that placed them in direct historical allegiance with the Three Musketeers and Zorro, was their swords.

One of their primary duties was to provide an honor escort for the bishop when he made his rounds to local parishes for confirmations and special occasions like the dedication of a new church or school or the graduation ceremony for a Catholic high school. They would arrive at the church in a sleek, black station wagon that followed the bishop's limousine.

"What a religion!" I often thought to myself as I watched the long, glimmering blades of the swords sway back and forth from the hips of the knights as they swaggered in front of the bishop in a pre-procession parade, walking from the bishop's parked car to the church while we altar boys watched from the sidewalk alongside the church where we were assembled, waiting to lead the procession ahead of the knights. No wonder that these sword-wielding Errol Flynn types did not escape our notice as we stood there, a pitiful little bunch dressed in short white surplices over black cassocks, an outfit that would have been unthinkable for a boy to wear in any other circumstance and which might be described by the untrained and irreligious as a woman's nightgown over a black housedress.

One year at confirmation, we all stood waiting for the

bishop to enter the church. One of the Knights of Columbus drew his sword in a particularly swashbuckling manner, prompting Edward Lilla, an altar boy with that most dangerous of attributes, a sense of humor, to yell, "Seize that man!" Edward hadn't seen Sister Leon standing behind the church pillar and was the most surprised person among us when she grabbed a good fistful of hair at the back of his neck and pulled him into the church. I don't remember much about Edward after that. He must have been reduced to a quiet, model student after the incident.

When the bishop, the knights, the parish priest, and the altar boys were all ready, the procession would begin. We'd enter the church to a soft, high organ march. Our priest, Father Fritz, waddled along behind the snaking line of altar boys arranged two by two (organized by height) until the last lanky eighth-graders loomed a full head and shoulders above the diminutive, dazed parson for whom their forward position was supposed to be a show of respect. We filed into the first three pews and were allowed to turn around so that we could watch the bishop come down the aisle.

First came the knights in their plumes and satin. They positioned themselves along the pews on each side of the aisle. Then when the bishop entered the vestibule at the back of church, they drew their swords, holding the hilts at chin level and extending the shiny metal high into the air, an honor salute as the prelate walked past. His Excellency took his time, walking slowly, solemnly, nodding his mitered head from side to side in acknowledgment of the devout presence of the hushed and adoring parishioners. His regal entrance was a wondrous sight seldom witnessed in modern democracies, and the homage and loyalty that it seemed to inspire among the adult congregation fired our imaginations in the manner of fairy tales and Arthurian legends. No wonder my Protestant friends, whose services to me always seemed like a combination of catechism class and a campfire sing-along, were always willing to come to church with me for the really big events. Of course, my evangelical efforts would be ultimately foiled. I wanted to convert these friends to Catholicism, but they were just coming for the spectacle. How could I blame them? Spring Grove didn't have the Roman Coliseum, but it had the Roman religion.

It was in the spring of eighth grade when Sister Leon announced that the Knights of Columbus were holding an essay contest on the subject of—what else?—Christopher Columbus's discovery of America. I figured that if those fellows with the giant ostrich feathers couldn't get me noticed, then no one could. I entered and won second place.

The first report I got from Sister Leon was that I had won first prize, and it wasn't until the actual awards ceremony that I learned otherwise. My response to her was immediate and base. "Two-hundred smackers?" I cried out on the playground where she gave me the news. This was the amount of the prize money. I was overwhelmed by the figure because it was almost as much money as my father made in a whole month.

The first hint that my recognition by this august and flamboyant group might not be as grand as I had hoped came as my parents and I entered the Knights of Columbus hall in Woodstock the evening of the awards presentation. A dimly lit room engulfed us along with the odor of cigars and stale beer. There was a dark, paneled wall hung with photos of softball teams, a couple of neon beer signs that depicted Wisconsin fishing lakes and waterfalls, and a faded green pool table. Three or four knights were belly up against a bar at one end of the hall having beers, hard-boiled eggs, and Slim Jims. Much to my amazement, they were wearing bowling shirts. I wondered where their fancy outfits might be.

The bartender turned away from the televised baseball game (the Cubs were playing the Dodgers) when he heard us slam the screen door. He looked at us for a long moment, then without speaking pointed toward the staircase that led to the basement. I was relieved that the ceremony wasn't going to be held in the bar, which seemed to be where the Knights of Columbus hung out when they were not with the bishop.

We had a dinner of pan-fried chicken, mashed potatoes and gravy, and canned peas and carrots. Not all that bad, I thought, though I noticed that the chicken was not quite as good as Mom's. My father always said, "No one can season chicken like your mother." I was hoping for some good apple pie, which usually followed our Sunday chicken dinners at home, but we each were offered a small scoop of lime sherbet in a little stainless steel dish instead. My mother said the coffee wasn't fresh.

The presentation followed the dinner. There was a group of middle-aged and older men at a head table. I assumed they were the knights in charge, even though they too were dressed in civilian clothes. The oldest of this group clicked his spoon against a glass and stood up. I thought to myself that surely now I would get noticed.

There were three winners: first, second, and third place.

To my great disappointment, the two-hundred-dollar first-prize money dropped to thirty-five dollars for second place and twenty-five dollars for third. I stood next to the elderly presenter, looking over his shoulder at the checks that he held. He had just awarded the third prize and was talking about my essay as he waved the check around. I could see the number "35" in the amount box of the next check, and felt sure that he was covering the "1" in front of the "35" with his thumb. He wasn't.

Things got worse as the evening wore on. The two other winners were going to go to the seminary to study for the priesthood. When this was announced you could hear a collective sigh of satisfaction, followed by thunderous ap-plause from the ranks of the nylon- and bowling-shirted knights, many of whom had wandered down to the banquet hall after the ball game. When my check was presented, however, the old knight announced that I would be attending Marian Central in Woodstock, a coeducational institution. This news was greeted by polite applause.

I've come to realize that the knights were spiritually nourished by their special connection to the bishop. It was his presence that allowed them to act out their particular brand of adoration, to stand at attention on either side of the church aisle, swords brandished, chins jutting, and plumed heads held high. When the bishop passed under their arc of steel, when he glided by noiselessly in his black patent leather Florsheims, they knew that he was the very embodiment of spiritual power and holiness. And to help send two young men to the seminary to study for this priesthood, to start these young Catholics on a course that might ultimately lead to the high office of bishop—well, it was a pleasure and thrill for the knights.

I was a different case, of course. I could hear the disappointment in their restrained applause, see it in their eyes. I was going to attend Marian Central, and they knew that there was no telling what kind of trouble a Catholic boy could get into with a school full of girls and thirty-five dollars in his pocket. So I never got properly noticed by the Knights of Columbus.

Two weeks later, I entered my freshman year. I thought that perhaps here at the Catholic high school I might receive some sort of special recognition for my runner-up essay, perhaps an all-school assembly or a special chapel, but there wasn't even an announcement after morning prayers.

It became clear to me after a few weeks of high school that certain students would be noticed and appreciated, especially by their peers. These were the ones who had come to school with friends, who had been in their elementary school student council and mission clubs, who had been playing tackle football together since sixth grade. I knew that I was destined to languish in relative social obscurity, which in fact I did for two or three years.

It was during my senior year that I began to see hope for a change in status. I made the first string of the football team, was elected to a secondary student council office, and I got into Sister Maria's history class.

Now, being vice-president of the student council was a pretty high honor for someone from St. Peter's, particularly since I was chosen for this post in an all-school election. However, like vice-presidents at every level, I lived in the shadow of our charismatic and witty student council president, whom I, coincidentally, played behind on the football team until he hurt his knee and I was thrust into the starting position at left guard. He was a very popular guy who had parlayed three years of being class clown and entertainer into the political coup of our senior year by winning the presidency of the student council as a dark horse.

As for the football team, I had a great time playing, and my teammates became my best friends. This was certainly the turning point of my high school experience as far as friendship went. But again, as any fan of football knows, playing left guard on the offensive line is no way to gain the notice of the fans or other students who are not directly involved in the game. It is very rare for an offensive lineman to even have his name mentioned at the game, other than during the announcement of starting lineups. The offensive backfield and ends who carried the ball got their names called all the time, of course, and the defensive players got their name announced over the public address system every time they made a tackle.

I did come pretty close to being a star once, at least for a moment. It was one of the biggest games of the year against our toughest opponent, Joliet Catholic, a school perennially recognized as having one of the best football teams in the state. At halftime, the score was tied. They had a dangerous halfback by the name of Ziegler who was small, shifty, and fast. He had been gaining a lot of yards on us in the first half. Coach said that he would probably be receiving the kickoff at the opening of the second half and that we should start things off right by "laying the wood" to him—in other words, hitting him hard.

I lined up on the kickoff team for the opening of the second half. This is the group that runs down the field after the ball is kicked off and tackles the ball carrier. I remember standing on the field as we were about to kick off. I looked around at the stadium. It was the largest I had ever seen, with tall, concrete bleachers that were filled with a couple thousand people. The autumn air was cool. I could smell the grass and the sweat off my uniform and I was with my friends. It was almost perfect except for the occasional realization that I might get killed by any one of several really big guys playing on the other side.

Our kicker set himself and raised his arm in the air, the referee blew his whistle to start the clock, and the game resumed. The kickoff sent the ball to about the one-yard line. Ziegler caught the ball there and headed up field. I played in the middle next to the kicker, so my job was to go right toward the ball carrier. It is always difficult and confusing to pick out the ball carrier from all the blockers, but as I dodged a couple of blocks a gap opened and I saw Ziegler cut sharply to the sideline. I turned too, heading right for the spot on the sideline where I knew he had to turn to cut upfield in order to keep from running out of bounds. Now those little halfbacks were usually great athletes, agile and quick, hard to catch. But when you finally tackled them, your size advantage came into play.

Ziegler had to hesitate and change his momentum as he made the turn. On the other hand, I was heading in a direct line for him with a pretty good head of steam. I probably outweighed him by twenty-five pounds and was a good five inches taller. When we collided he got the worst of it. I hardly felt any impact at all, just a release underneath me like a wave crashing at the seashore. We rolled over together two or three times and came to a stop. The ref blew the whistle to signal the end of the play. I had stopped him on the eighteen-yard line. It was the best open field tackle I had ever made. As I returned to the bench and to the awaiting gratitude of my coach I practiced my best strutting trot, with my ears tuned to the public address announcer who said in a loud, clear voice, "Tackled by Redlin." The announcer had confused my number with someone else's. At that moment, I concluded that I would never be noticed. It just wasn't in the cards.

But at least I was in Sister Maria's history class that year. I loved history, and everyone loved Sister Maria. She made an impression the first day I met her. She was of heroic stature, probably a good bit over six feet tall. Now the Sisters of The Holy Cross wore long black gowns with large white collars and a round, dish-like halo at the back of their heads. The halo was made out of a kind of cardboard material so it looked like they were wearing corrugated Frisbees. It was difficult for a woman of average height to look distinguished or even professional in such an outfit, but not for Sister Maria. She would stride down the school hall, taking long steps, her gown hanging gracefully on her tall, slender torso. When she turned and smiled, her sharp facial features and accompanying halo atop her black robe, she seemed to me like some oriental painting of a graceful crane caught in the foreground of a great full moon. Her eyes were a light blue and her skin rosy and pure, the "map of Ireland" all over her face.

Each day, after school was dismissed, she accumulated a large gathering of students who flocked around her desk at the front of the room. Since she taught upperclassmen, this phenomenon was something that every freshman and sophomore watched with envy each day for a couple of years before getting a chance to be among her admirers.

I joined this group my last year in high school by taking her senior history class. It didn't take me long to understand why everyone wanted to be in her class. She loved history and never seemed to tire of the subject or her students. She encouraged us to ask questions and draw our own conclusions. We also did a lot of role-playing. I remember that certain students in class got to act out the Sacco and Vanzetti trial. We had a mock political convention and also history trivia contests. This was where I intended to shine, to be noticed by Sister Maria.

One Monday in September, she announced that we would have a trivia contest the following Friday. The topic was World War I. I studied hard. I read everything in our text and even looked up additional information at the library. I had friends read me the study questions from the back of the book. By Friday I was ready. I figured I knew everything that was worth knowing about the war in question.

The way the quiz worked was that Sister could ask any question about the subject. The first person to stand and say the answer got ten points. If you stood up and didn't know the answer you lost twenty points. Friday came and the game was on. Sister asked the first question: "What event precipitated World War I?"

In a second I flashed on the answer and at the same time upon my good fortune at knowing the very first question stone cold. It was easy. The answer was the assassination of Franz Ferdinand, the nephew of the emperor of Austria. He was gunned down in Sarajevo, in the area known as the Balkan peninsula.

Filled with confidence and the knowledge that I would soon show Sister Maria what a scholar and all-around knowledgeable guy I could be, I jumped to my feet before anyone else had a chance to move and shouted, "Franz Joseph's nephew Franz Ferdinand was shot in the Balkans!"

Something seemed wrong. There was no reaction from my rivals indicating that I had given the correct answer. No applause or cheering, just a stunned silence. And then laughter, uproarious laughter. Somewhere between the second and third wave of laughter I realized what I had said—or more precisely, the additional meaning of what I had said.

I began to laugh, too, trying to disguise my embarrassment and humiliation. I had wanted to impress Sister Maria, but instead, I had said something offensive, even sexual. I thought I would never be able to look her in the eye again. I stood there at my desk, staring at the blackboard. She always stood in the back of the room during these quizzes. I didn't want to turn around. I didn't want to see her disappointment, her disapproval.

But I knew that I had to face her. So as I sat back down in my seat, I turned toward the back of the room. There she was, holding her stomach, all six foot three inches of her bent over, laughing, God bless her.

Four years later, I graduated from the University of Illinois. The Vietnam War was raging and I was teaching elementary school. I was given a teaching deferment by my local draft board, renewable on a year-to-year basis. I had studied history and political science in college and was convinced that the Vietnam War was an unjust conflict that our political leaders did not understand, and that the lives lost on both sides were a tragic waste. Gradually my thinking began to shift to the possibility that all war was useless. I began reading books about the pacifist nature of the New Testament. Finally I decided to give up my teaching deferment and apply for official status as a conscientious objector. This was less courageous than it might have been because the draft board had gone to a lottery system, the war was winding down, and it did not appear that my relatively high lottery number, 191, would be called. In any event, I thought the logical thing for me to do was to apply for reclassification.

One of the application requirements was the submission of letters from authority figures—teachers, priests, ministers, community leaders—who could attest to the applicant's long-standing religious and ethical beliefs. It was not enough if a person had just recently decided that they did not want to kill or be killed.

In assembling a batch of letters to document my sincerity, I thought it would be important to have a letter from one of my high school teachers. It took a bit of trial and error, but I finally located Sister Maria working in a war-on-poverty program in Hammond, Indiana. After going through several layers of phone extensions peopled with businesslike voices, I recognized her voice. A bit flustered, I tried to identify myself.

"Hello, Sister, this is Jim May from Woodstock, Illinois. You remember, ah, it was Marian Central Catholic High School, ah, in the early sixties. Ah, I was in your history class in about 1965. Remember? Jim May? Marian Central?"

There was a short silence at the other end of the line.

"Oh yes! Jim May, shot in the Balkans!"

So I guess I finally did get noticed by Sister Maria, after all.

A Bell For Shorty

*M*y father's nickname was Shorty. He wasn't particularly short, but he was the second son born to a farm
family of twelve children, and when his oldest brother, my
uncle Ben, gave him the nickname, it stuck. In our small
town there were many nicknames: Happy Wagoner,
Squirrelly Ashe, Skunk Adams, and Jerky John. Given the
range of possible friendly appellations, "Shorty" wasn't
so bad, I suppose, and my father never complained. As I
grew up, it never occurred to me that his nickname had
anything to do with his height. It was simply what most
people called my father. Our family called him Dad.

My father was fifty-one years old when I was born; my
mother was forty-two. They were devout Roman Catholics
and I was a "rhythm baby." My mother used to say that all
Catholics were preoccupied with two things, rhythm and
bingo, and if the rhythm didn't work, bingo! I was a bingo.

The best thing about being the youngest was the year I
had my father all to myself. I was five years old, and there
was no kindergarten at the one-room school I would attend
the following fall. My oldest sister was married and my other

two sisters were in high school. My brother was working construction, and my mother assembled typewriters at a factory in Woodstock. Each day, after an enormous farm breakfast of bacon, sausage, fried potatoes, eggs, pancakes, and German coffeecake, everyone scattered to their destinations in town, leaving Dad and me, the oldest and the youngest, at home to be the real farmers.

He and I went everywhere together: to the barn, out to the fields to plow and plant, and on visits to his horse-trading buddies. Visits to these traders were my favorites, because they usually meant a longer drive than just stopping by a neighbor's farm.

We loved car rides. After milking was done we'd get into the Chevrolet Bel Air and head out, sometimes driving in excess of thirty-five miles per hour; my father was born in 1896 and was most comfortable at carriage speeds. I'd kneel on the front seat so that I could lean my arm out the passenger window, and Dad would light up a cigar.

Our dog, Bootsie, loved these trips, too. Farm dogs are usually big, tough, and shaggy, but my father loved to crossbreed rat terriers with Chihuahuas. Bootsie was the outcome of this genetic horseplay—what we called a "lap-yap." But she was tough. She chased cows—would get right after them and bite their heels. The cows would kick right over the top of her, so it worked out pretty well. Once, though, we had a brindle cow that kicked straight out like a mule. Her hoof caught Bootsie right between the eyes and punted her through the air like a football. She landed with a sickening thud and lay still. I put her in a burlap bag and dragged her all the way home, which probably didn't do her any good.

That night I put the sack at the end of the bed and cried myself to sleep. We all figured she was dead. The next morning she jumped out of the sack and trotted all over the house, just as easy as you please. The blow even cleared up a disgusting nasal snort that she had had all her life—an effective cure, perhaps, but not one recommended for less hardy creatures.

As the car rolled steadily and determinedly toward our destination, Bootsie would jump down from the front seat onto the floor, scurry under the springs and cushions to the back, jump up onto the back seat, leap high onto the backrest of the front seat, and perch for a precarious moment. She'd then hurl herself through the air, landing on the front bench seat, and springboard to the floor once again to repeat the ritual.

With Dad driving at modest speed, she could accomplish this cycle approximately six times per mile. Her moments on top of the front seat were critical, since any bump in the road or one of Dad's frequent steering adjustments could send her on a scrambling freefall backwards onto the floor; a sudden braking of the car would vault her, rocketlike, toward the dashboard, ears flattened against the sides of her head, a half-bark, half-scream emitting, Doppler-like, from her tiny mouth as she sailed through our field of vision voicing the extreme displeasure with which she greeted her impending and eventual collision with the windshield. The possibility of her being skewered by the Jesus icon mounted on the dashboard was an ever-present fear of mine that never materialized.

We must have been quite a sight, traveling a serpentine route at sub-automobile speeds in a rusty green Chevrolet—a grandfatherly figure wearing a straw fedora, smoking a cigar, and scanning the pastures and woodlots earnestly for signs of a horse that might be for sale; a small boy with a seemingly elongated upper torso that allowed his arm to hang out the window in a haughty, adult fashion; and the dark blur of a small dog going around and around hamsterlike, with such intensity that she appeared to be propelling the vehicle at its leisurely pace.

Dad's horse-trading friends included a wide assortment

of men, his age and older, whose ability to bargain, persuade, entertain, connive, and yes, swindle (in a friendly sort of way) allowed them to live at the edge and apart from the daily rounds of the tiring, bone-numbing work that was the lot of most dairy farmers. These traders always seemed good-humored and in the mood to stop whatever they were doing on their place when Dad and I pulled into their yards. I came to learn that this was due in part to my father's own wit and charm, but also to the relish with which these rough-necked dealers welcomed the chance to talk about their favorite horses, their best trades, and the general outrageousness of the lives that they led.

My early years were filled with long afternoons in cold, pungent barns, sitting on hay bales and listening to stories and anecdotes punctuated by the snorting and hoof-stomping of horses in their adjoining stalls. The stories were generally along the lines of trading a blind horse for a dry cow, and who got the better of the deal.

I went along to work in the fields, too. I remember sitting with Dad high up on the iron seat of the old tractor, the big seat with the holes drilled in it for the rainwater to drain through. There was plenty of room for both of us on that wide, flat, piece of iron. I sat half in his lap, surrounded by his arms as he held the steering wheel. Sometimes I'd grab the wheel and "help" him steer. Other times I'd watch intently as the plow cut through the ground and the ground responded: slowly turning over itself, exposing the rich loamy soil, the dark flesh of the prairie, where each year farmers planted their seeds and hopes. Most times I would just daydream while holding onto my father's arms, enjoying the smell of sweat and Old Spice.

In late summer, as we made our way toward the house at noon or at the end of the day, we would often stop the tractor under the chokecherry tree that grew along the fence line. We could reach the cherries from the seat. We'd sit for a long time and eat them. They don't call them chokecherries for nothing. They were bittersweet at best, with a large stone in the middle. But I loved sitting there in the shade of that scallop-barked tree with its delicate, shiny leaves, eating something wild that I had picked myself. My father always knew where to forage for food. We'd pick asparagus in the spring and hickory nuts in the fall. Having grown up on a tenant farm with eleven brothers and sisters, he never took any food for granted, particularly if it was provided by nature without requirement of cash or toil.

During those quiet times under the chokecherry tree, we'd listen for the sound of the meadowlark calling from its perch on a fence post or a bobolink singing on the wing as it flew over the clover and alfalfa. Dad could make a whistling sound that he told me was the call of a bobwhite quail. I never heard a quail answer nor did I ever see one, as they were pretty well hunted-out in those days. But years later, I was in Virginia one afternoon and I heard a low, clear whistle from a woodlot. I recognized the sound instantly. It sounded like Shorty May.

In those days, even though I was five years old, I never thought of myself as being "babysat." I was the official "hooker-upper" on the place, and could drive a tractor, in a manner of speaking. In late summer the corn stood tall in the fields but was still green and juicy. We'd hook up a hay wagon to the tractor. I'd lift the wagon tongue (most were four-wheeled in those days, so there was no weight on the tongue) while Dad backed the tractor toward me. When the coupling hole in the tractor's drawbar matched the hole in the wagon tongue, I'd drop a pin through both holes, joining the wagon and tractor. I was proud of this contribution because I knew that it would have been nearly impossible for my dad to do that job alone. Next we'd pull the wagon down to the cornfield, cut and load some corn, and feed it to the cows when they came up to the barn for milking.

My job was to "drive" the tractor while Dad cut the corn. Once we reached the cornfield, he'd put the tractor in first gear and hold the clutch pedal to the floor. Then I'd put my small work shoe on top of his heavy work boot, and while the tractor continued to run he would slowly slide his foot out from under mine. I could feel the tension of the clutch pedal rising against my foot and as I pushed back with all my weight, the pedal would slowly depress again. At that moment I took control of the big machine.

While I watched from the tractor seat, Dad would take a wooden-handled corn knife from a toolbox on the wagon and begin cutting the tall stalks of corn, swinging the knife in slow, steady arcs. The stalks would tremble as the knife passed through them, hesitate for a moment, and then lie down into the crook of his arm. When he had a pretty good bunch of stalks, he'd throw the bundle onto the wagon. As he worked his way across the field row by row, he'd get quite a distance away from me and the wagon—too far to carry the heavy bundle of corn. This was the moment I waited for, the chance to prove myself. He'd turn toward me and the tractor, quickly gauge the distance as being too much, and holler, "Go!"

I'd let up ever so slowly on the clutch. If my foot slipped off the pedal at this juncture the clutch plate would catch all at once, engaging the engine; the tractor would rear up onto its big, black, back tires like a red metal stallion, land with a clank, and kill the engine; and I would have failed, for the time being, at my quest to be a real, grown-up farmer.

Usually, I'd be able to let the clutch out slowly enough that the tractor would creep ahead, in a kind of jerky, halting sort of a way, to where Dad was standing with the corn, until he hollered, "Whoa!" Then I'd push the clutch pedal down and let out a sigh of satisfaction as he tossed the corn onto the wagon. I was pleased that I had saved him a lot of time and effort walking back and forth to the wagon and climbing on and off the tractor to move it closer to his work. He was nearly sixty years old and farming three hundred acres by himself; even then I was aware of his age and how hard he worked.

There were times when I couldn't go along with him, times when I had to stay alone back at the house. There was the time that I rang the bell.

It was early May, corn-planting time. The McHenry County farmers say you plant your corn "when the oak leaves are the size of a squirrel's ear." It was in the early morning on a soft spring day—a planting day. I had awakened to the sound of robins and the smell of plowed earth coming through my open bedroom window. The birds were back and the lilacs, planted carefully to the south of the house, perfumed the breeze, which was carrying spring all the way from the Gulf of Mexico. I watched Dad milk and feed the cows, helped him hook up the corn planter, and looked on as he filled first the canisters that held the fertilizer and then the ones that contained the corn seed itself. When he was finished and had tightened the last wing nut on the last bolt, he looked at me, thought for a moment, and said as he turned toward the tractor, "You'll have to stay home today."

I didn't understand why. It seemed like a horrible injustice. Looking back, I think he may have been afraid to have me sitting with him on the tractor seat that day. There was a lot of moving around when you planted corn. We used an ancient two-row planter that had been converted from horse-drawn to mechanical. A man sitting on the tractor had to reach around and back to put the planter in gear by hand. The marker arms had to be lifted and dropped again at the end of every pass so that each row of corn was properly spaced for future cultivating and harvesting. With all that movement, a small boy could easily be bumped and fall under the tractor wheel. Farming is dangerous work. Every farmer knew a friend or relative who had lost a hand or an arm to a machine. Local accounts of some child crushed under the wheel of a tractor or truck served as moral lessons and cautionary tales.

Before he got on the tractor, Dad turned to me and said, "I know you'll be alone, so if there's trouble, ring the bell."

A rusty, cinnamon-colored bell hung from a wooden frame on the roof of a storage shed we called the shanty. The shanty was attached to the house. I had never heard the bell.

A greasy, hemp rope fell from the bell to a thick knot that was tied to some rafters. That morning, Dad had climbed a ladder up to the rafters to untie the rope. It had uncoiled and danced its way down, almost touching the ground.

"It's not for fun or foolishness, but if there's trouble, ring the bell. I'll hear it in the field and come back in on the tractor."

He left for the field. I watched the tractor roll down the lane, getting smaller and smaller. Finally it was out of sight. I didn't like being there alone. I was afraid someone might come down the driveway. It wasn't just strangers that scared me. I was just plain shy, frightened even of neighbors. I had many four-legged friends, and two-legged friends with feathers, but I wasn't used to being around people.

The time was passing ever so slowly, so I thought I'd go into the shanty to play. It was an interesting old building that had been built originally for carriages. It was much too narrow for the big cars we had in the fifties. (Now these buildings have cars parked in them all the time. They've gone from buggies to Toyotas!) Back then we used the shanty to store odds and ends: bald tires, old harnesses and license plates nailed to the wall. I liked to go in there to look around. I could usually find some greasy, rusty thing to take apart and, occasionally, put back together. So it was with a mild sense of adventure that I entered the dusty old building that day.

When my eyes had adjusted to the darkness, I saw our dog, Bootsie, asleep in a dirt hole. Curled up next to her was a snake. This snake looked threatening, and I had overheard some talk about rattlesnakes on neighbors' farms. Recalling my father's words, I thought to myself, *This could be trouble.* I looked up at the bell. I liked the idea of ringing it. I liked the idea of Dad coming in early from the field. I knew he'd be coming in for the noon meal, which we called dinner, but it was still mid-morning and I didn't want to wait. I looked at the snake again and it seemed to have gotten bigger, with a more sinister look on its face. I thought, *This is trouble enough.*

I grabbed the old hemp rope and gave it a pull that literally lifted my feet off the ground. When the side of the rusty bell hit the clapper, it sent a low, rich toll out over the fields. The pigeons flew up off the barn and the young heifers jumped around in the pasture with their tails straight in the air. I guess they had never heard the bell either. I liked the sound so much that I gave it another pull.

When the toll had drifted away, I heard something else: the engine of my father's tractor. Every tractor sounds different. This was his. He had heard the bell and was coming in from the field.

It wasn't long before a buoyant, sooty line of exhaust smoke appeared over the corncrib, and then I saw Dad wheeling the tractor around the corner of the toolshed, really moving. He had the old International H tractor in "road gear." It was unusual for him to drive that fast. He had farmed most of his life with horses—heavily muscled Percherons and Belgians, with feet as big as serving platters and withers as high as a man's forehead. He loved those big horses and used to train the raw, young ones to pull together in a harness and work at a farmer's side. But he never quite trusted tractors and machinery. He drove slowly on these metal beasts—second or third gear. So that day when I saw his tractor belching smoke and coming into the yard at full speed, I knew that he was worried about me and I thought, *Maybe I am in trouble!*

The tractor braked, coming to a stop right in front of me. He turned the engine off and it got real quiet, the kind of stillness only noticed after it has been preceded by a loud noise. "What's the trouble?" he asked, still seated on the tractor.

"There's a snake over there by Bootsie!" I replied, pointing to the shanty. He climbed down off the tractor and walked quickly to the old building, taking big steps. I followed behind him, running. It turned out to be a garter snake, about eight inches long and disappointingly harmless. He let go with a big sigh like he was relieved that I was safe and sound. Then he got mad.

For parents fearful of their children's safety, life is an emotional seesaw. As soon as they find out the kids are alive, they want to kill them.

"I've got a lot of planting to do today. I can't be coming back in unless its more trouble than that!" He turned toward the house, walking past me, muttering that I was "bugs," which was pretty strong language for him. That was the last he said about the incident.

We had our dinner early that day. He stayed long enough to hear the noon farm report on the radio. He even listened to a little bit of the music that came on the Chicago Barn Dance station after the news. But he didn't dance that day. Most times when the music came on, he'd do a little fox trot across the linoleum floor—dance to the radio in his worn overalls with the cool breeze blowing under the maples and through the kitchen window, until it was time to go back to the hot, dusty field. He didn't dance that day, so I suppose he was more angry with me than he let on, and I never rang the bell again.

The following year, on the first of March, we auctioned

the farming business and moved to town. Dad said it was because of the price of milk and the recession. I think the work was getting too hard for him.

March first is the day that farm leases are up. A tenant farmer can move and be settled in time to get the crop in. But this time we moved to town. There would be no crop, no planting or harvest to mark our lives, no cows for Dad to milk and feed twice a day. We kept a couple of horses and my pony, which we pastured at a neighbor's, and sold everything else.

On the day of the sale, Dad woke me early. He walked into my bedroom while it was still dark. "Do you wanna go with me to feed the heifers? It will probably be the last time."

We went together. I've always been grateful that I worked with him on the last day that we were farmers together. It's the only thing I remember about the sale.

He got a job working in a milk machine factory in town. It must have been hard on him working inside after all those years of farming, but he never said too much about it. The second spring in town, he was laid off from the factory and was hired to work on a Lipizzan horse farm. This was a blessing because he loved horses. He cared for the brood mares, and I would go with him to help on weekends, especially in the wintertime when the mares "came due." Sometimes we'd sit up together all night. Over the years we welcomed many slippery, spindly-legged foals into the world. We were partners again in the farming business.

One day while I was at school, he was leading a big stallion across a hayfield to a new barn when the big horse bolted. The stud horse threw its head, jerking on the leather lead that Dad was holding. I remember him saying, "If I would have let go, I would have been all right." Instead he'd held on and fought the horse. Maybe he'd remembered his younger days, cowboying those raw, young draft horses that he had trained to behave and work at a farmer's side. But Dad was old now, and the strain was too much. He had a heart attack and died a short time later. I was sixteen.

In the years that followed, there were times in my life when there was trouble, and I ached to pull on the rope, but I didn't have a bell to ring and he didn't have a tractor to drive in from the field.

This story has been silent for years, like the old bell. But now when I tell it, it feels to me like I'm pulling on the rope. And if you hear that bell, or maybe a bell of your own, then I know I've rung it. Shorty May taught me to listen to the land and to its people, and sometimes while searching my memories, I can hear the tractor coming, too.